A LUELLA VAN HORN MYSTERY

MURDER ON SEX ISLAND

JO FIRESTONE

Murder on Sex Island
A Luella van Horn Mystery

©2023 Jo Firestone

print ISBN: 979-8-35091-491-7
ebook ISBN: 979-8-35091-492-4

"Watch as thirty sexy singles come together to decide who's the best at sex. The winners get $100,000 and the losers get humiliated. Only on Sex Island!"

-The introductory narration for every episode of Sex Island

"I'd rather be dead than sing "Satisfaction" when I'm 45."

-Mick Jagger

CAST OF CHARACTERS

Marie Jones — *A mousy ex-social worker divorcée from Staten Island desperately trying to reinvent herself as sexy private detective, Luella van Horn. Lives in Manhattan with two cats. She's a big Sex Island fan and your narrator.*

Sophie — *Marie Jones' curmudgeonly next-door neighbor. A reluctant cat-sitter.*

Tasha — *A Sex Island contestant with doe eyes and very long black hair. A very recent ex of David G's.*

Blair — *A Sex Island contestant known for her cruelty. A recent ex of David G's. Currently paired with Nate.*

Sarah — *A Sex Island contestant know for being ~~bland~~ kind. Tall, blonde, and currently paired with David N. Another recent ex of David G's.*

Nate — *The only Christian Sex Island contestant. Best friend to David G. Currently paired with Blair. It need not be mentioned, but he does have six-pack abs.*

David G — *A beloved Sex Island contestant from Philadelphia. Previously a nurse. Brother to Francis. Most recently paired with Tasha.*

David N — A Sex Island contestant known for being a reliable rebound. Very skinny and desperately trying to grow a goatee. Currently paired with Sarah.

Ethan — A Sex Island contestant with anger issues, originally from Kansas. Short and hairy, he has a reputation for being enormously endowed.

Phil — A Sex Island contestant from Wisconsin. Vapid, beautiful, and prefers to keep to himself.

Stephanie Hillson — A long-time executive producer on Sex Island. A mother of two children and recently single.

John Murphy — A first-time executive producer on Sex Island. Originally from Philadelphia. Nervous and talkative.

George Striker — The director of Sex Island. A sleaze bag known for his bottomless piña colada policy and mostly unbuttoned shirts.

Isa — A hard-working, underpaid production assistant on Sex Island who sees everything.

AJ — A wild card contestant on Sex Island. A big fan of the New York Jets.

Justin — Another wild card contestant. Identifies as a triple threat: model, actor, and model consultant.

Lauren — An old friend of Marie Jones' from Staten Island.

Sheila — A naturopath and on-set medic who believes in the healing powers of raw garlic.

Max — A sound guy on Sex Island who hears everything.

Francis — David G's older sister.

Detective Johannes — A helpful local detective with a significant mustache.

1

Like my forefathers, Gene Simmons and Christina Aguilera, my life began in Staten Island, the borough of New York most known for its landfills. The first 25 years of my life were going somewhat according to plan. I was an underpaid social worker, I got married to a man I knew from high school, and to top it all off, I was dead inside. What can I say? It's the Staten Island way.

When most grown people get bored, they cheat on their spouses. They start buying lottery tickets. They develop a drug habit. Not me, though. No, sir. When I need to fill a gaping void in an otherwise predictable, monotonous life, I like to think outside the box. So I made up an alter ego named Luella van Horn who solves crimes. Is that the worst thing in the world? In theory, no.

When I slap on a blonde wig, fake white teeth, and some red lipstick, I become Private Detective Luella van Horn. Suddenly I'm a woman who knows what she wants and gets it. People start paying attention to me. They tell me things they're not supposed to. The powerful see me as an ally and the weak see me as a threat. It's amazing. I think it's probably because of the teeth.

Growing up, all I wanted was to be someone like Luella van Horn. To have people finally look at me like I have something to offer. Something they want.

When you're mousy, nobody cares where you're going at night. When you come back to the house at 2 a.m., and your husband sleepily asks, "Were you gone?" you can say, "No," and he'll believe you, turn over, and go right back to sleep. Nobody bothers to ask why you're spending thousands of dollars on blonde wigs (made with real human hair!), and going to the dentist for teeth molds, and maxing out your credit cards at Sephora. They've barely noticed.

I began Luella's private detective agency a little over four years ago. The cases were small to start, like who stole the cookie from the cookie jar? (As it turns out, it was the local police commissioner.) I ruffled feathers here and there, but only enough to get a certain amount of notoriety around Staten Island. The local blogs described Luella as intuitive, smart, and savvy. A rising star private detective. A bombshell. Me! A *bombshell*! In retrospect, I'd been lucky. Then the Bell case happened.

It was around this time, the whole double-life shtick had started to wear me down. My husband was becoming suspicious. He couldn't understand why there wasn't a hot dinner on the table every night. Things were getting a little tense in our marriage. I'd hurry home after a long day of social work, make him a dry pork chop, grab my duffle bag and change in the car. Then Luella would take it from there. I was tired but I was happy. I was simply not prepared for the monster that is Taylor Bell.

If you only read the news reports, you'd think Luella van Horn was good at her job. You wouldn't know she almost convicted the wrong man, nearly lost her social worker's license, and essentially ruined her marriage. All the papers said was, thanks to the elusive Luella van Horn, Taylor Bell was now in jail awaiting trial for murdering his wife. That was enough to comfort the masses. Gotta love lazy journalism.

After the Bell case, I kept thinking what it would be like to be Luella full-time. Maybe I wouldn't mess up so much if I wasn't stretched so thin doing two jobs, living two lives. Soon after that, I left my husband and decided to quit social work altogether. I moved to Manhattan with what was left of my savings, turned 29, and adopted a cat. And then another cat. To keep the first cat company, of course. Using this logic, I understood how quickly someone could end up with forty cats in a one-bedroom apartment. To keep the other thirty-nine company. Duh.

So, now I exist as two women. One is who I've been most of my life: Marie Jones. A mousy ex-social worker divorcée with frizzy brown hair and an addiction to bad reality TV. The other is Luella van Horn. A glamorous private detective who has yet to find a case she couldn't solve, even if it was messy as hell. It's like I'm Sherlock and Watson rolled up in one. I am jealous Sherlock had a friend to take notes.

The hope is that I can one day leave Marie Jones by the wayside, exist only as Luella van Horn. I guess time will tell. That Staten Island Ferry runs to Manhattan a little more regularly than I would like.

TUESDAY

This particular case began like most of them do. With a missing person. New York City hadn't seen the likes of Luella van Horn for a while. There were small cases here and there, but after the Bell case, I felt like I needed a breather. I usually told callers Luella was on an extended vacation in the Keys. This translated to me sitting in my apartment talking to my cats (named Meatloaf and Meatball, if you're curious) and watching *Sex Island* like it was a religion.

If you're not familiar, *Sex Island* is an incredible reality television show. They take the country's sexiest 22-year-olds and fly them to a tropical paradise, while we, the viewers, watch them have sex and emotionally destroy each other. I don't know why or how the FCC allows them to broadcast intercourse, but I'm not going to be the one to raise a red flag. Maybe because the contestants are always under the covers? Who knows!

The show was somehow both addictive and completely unwatchable. There is something oddly comforting about sequestering our nation's sexually active youth to a land mass in the middle of the ocean. It aired every night for one full hour, and the ratings were, as you might imagine, very high. I did my part.

This season of *Sex Island* was quite compelling already. Every night, there was sex, screaming, fighting, and more sex. I mean, what more could one ask for. Smell-o-vision?

Each season of *Sex Island* started out with fifteen men and fifteen women, all straight, all cis-gendered, all 19 to 23 years old. This was the type of show where a 25-year-old was considered geriatric. As the season progressed, contestants were eliminated for anything really, from not having sex "good enough" to having an odd-smelling anus. Sure it was dystopian, but have you watched the news recently? It's about on par with the news. Suffice it to say, as Marie, I wasn't in a great place emotionally, financially, or otherwise.

The last two episodes of *Sex Island* had gotten strange. My favorite cast member, David G, was suddenly absent. No other cast members had addressed it, which was even more off-putting. Cast members would frequently leave the show, but their exodus would be decided upon by the group. Plus, it would be all anyone could talk about the next day in their confessionals. The last contestant to tearfully leave the show of her own accord was a professional cheerleader from Dallas,

Texas named Rachel. The show's official statement: *Rachel suffers from Crohn's Disease. We wish her well.*

I wasn't the only one to notice David G was gone. The message boards were abuzz — kidnapping was a popular theory, but one Reddit user was adamant she'd seen him in her local grocery store in Tampa, Florida. Another commenter claimed he was sending her signals through her air fryer. This is all to say the show had a very devoted following and David G was a unanimous favorite.

Before his disappearance, David G had been sleeping with a contestant named Tasha, a tall woman with long black hair who hated "wearing clothes." In the most recent episode, Tasha had been acting very strange. Take this little nugget from her confessional that had the *Sex Island* fans reeling:

Off-Camera Interviewer: Are you okay?

Tasha: Bitch, shut up!

I had a feeling something weird had happened, and usually — sadly — I'm not wrong about this stuff. David G was a rare type of contestant, in that he was hot, but he also seemed like he had a soul. He was called David G because there was another David on *Sex Island* called David N, and let me tell you, David N could not hold a candle to David G. Anyway, it might have been his cleft chin or his close-cut beard or the fact that he was a nurse before becoming a reality TV star — whatever it was, David G was a straight-up catch, and his absence was extremely noticeable.

I remember very clearly the night I got the call. I'd just poured myself a second bowl of generic Frosted Flakes. Technically it was my fifth bowl of the day but my second *after-dinner bowl*. I had taken a very large bite just as the phone started ringing. I chewed and looked at the phone, milk spilling down my chin. *No Caller ID.* I knew what that usually meant: a case. I looked to Meatloaf, the more spiritual of my two cats. His green eyes said, *Answer it.* I picked up on the third ring.

"Hello," I said with a mouth full of cereal.

"Is this Luella van Horn?" a man's voice asked.

I managed to chew and swallow. "This is her secretary. I can take a message," I said, coughing up a rogue flake. It landed gracefully on my couch cushion. I picked it up and ate it again. Meatloaf stared at me in horror.

"Uh, this is strictly confidential but I work as a producer on the reality show, *Sex Island,* and we'd like Ms. Van Horn to look into the disappearance of one of our cast members. His name is David G," the man said.

I bit down on my knuckle and kicked my legs. The cats darted away from me. Internally, I was squealing. A case on *Sex Island*? Was I dreaming?!

Externally, I oh-so-calmly replied, "Okay. And what's your name?" I was met with silence on the other end. Finally, the man spoke. "My name is John. Uh, John Murphy."

"So, John Murphy, when was David G last seen?" I asked.

"It's been about 48 hours," John said. "Can Luella come track him down? Is she available?" There was a growing urgency in his voice.

A second producer spoke up then. Already, she seemed more confident than John, less shaken.

"Hi there, I'm Stephanie Hillson, another executive producer on the show. Listen, we've scoured the island. We've talked to the cast and crew. Nobody knows anything. Which leaves us between a rock and a hard place."

"We've done everything we could other than contact his family and call the police. We just don't want to alarm anyone unnecessarily, you know? His family would be hysterical," John added.

"And of course, the viewers…" I added sarcastically.

"Yes, the viewers are our number one priority," Stephanie agreed.

I hoped she was joking, but it didn't seem that she was. I'd say, off the top of my head, the two main things you're supposed to do at a workplace when an employee disappears is contact their family and the police. But this was Hollywood, baby, and I knew they did things differently over there.

They'd heard Luella van Horn was the person to call when you wanted crimes solved quickly and quietly. That was the big one — quietly. With the ratings so high, John and Stephanie didn't think police interference was necessary at this point, but they wanted the problem solved.

"We're certain it's simply a matter of David G hiding somewhere," Stephanie insisted.

"Right. Sometimes, these actor-types really do take off for a few days! They only tell the PA, who forgets to tell us, and then they come back. And everyone's okay! For all we know, David G is suntanning on a boat somewhere right now." John chuckled nervously at his own joke. I noticed Stephanie didn't join him.

David G was a frontrunner on *Sex Island,* and his star was on the rise. If he was hiding, there had to be a really good reason for it. John and Stephanie hoped Luella could do some hush-hush private investigating, find David G alive and well, and be on her merry way. You might be wondering how someone could actually disappear in the age of social media. Well, the geniuses running *Sex Island* had a moratorium on posting, liking, and even sharing during the filming months, and that applied to all cast and crew. In fact, all contact with the outside world had been actively discouraged. David G's (and everyone else's) social media had been untouched for weeks.

"How much will you pay?" I asked.

For some reason, it was always easier to ask about money when it was for Luella. The producers got cagey but said they'd make it "very worth her while," plus a first-class ticket both ways. They asked if she could get to the island by tonight, as time was of the essence. I said I would relay the message and get back to them after I'd spoken to Luella. I hung up the phone and took the next three minutes to jump around my apartment screaming. Meatball hid under the bed while Meatloaf hissed at me from on top of a book shelf.

I know most sane people would ignore this vague offer with no concrete money on the table. They'd go on with their regular, sanity-drenched lives. But seeing as my life actually revolved around watching a reality show that was now a potential crime scene, I felt that doing something was the right thing to do. Call me an angel from heaven. An angel tracking down the very attractive David G on the set of her favorite television show. This could be the turning point I'd been hoping for. If Luella could solve this case, I might become so busy, I'd never have to live as Marie another day in my life.

I called them back. John picked up after the first ring.

"Hello? Did you talk to Luella?"

"She'll do it," I said.

"Amazing! Okay, just book her on the next first class ticket out — we'll wire you the money now."

I thanked him, then promptly got an airplane ticket that left New York in two hours and cost approximately $14 million dollars.

There was so much to do in so little time. Next, I called my 75-year-old neighbor, Sophie.

"Sophie, hi, how are you?"

"Cut the small talk." Sophie cleared her throat and spit up a loogie, which thanks to advanced technology, I could hear very clearly. "What do you want?!" she screeched.

If you can believe it, she was *always* this pleasant.

"Could you take care of my cats for a bit?"

She coughed twice directly into the receiver. "How long this time?"

"Not sure. Maybe two weeks, maybe a little more."

She treated me to another throat clear and then a very wet-sounding snort. "Alright. Have a bottle of Baileys waiting for me in the fridge."

"Always," I said.

If anyone in the city knew of my double identity, it was likely Sophie "Wet Snort" DePlaza. But she never said a word about it and neither did I. Is that considered a friendship?

With the cats taken care of, I took a shower, which was something I hadn't done in some time. Seeing as I was going to visit a tropical island, I tried to remove as much of my body hair as possible, but in my haste, there was no telling which tufts I missed.

Next, I put on my Luella face — red lipstick, a blonde wig, a smokey eye, and a set of fake, white teeth. I've always had a chipped front tooth, which is a lot like a car accident — nobody can stop themselves from staring at it. Wearing the perfect Luella teeth changes my whole face. Putting a nice blonde wig over the frizzy brown curls doesn't hurt, either. It's not that my goal is to be pretty, but I have found pretty gets you places plain wouldn't dream of. What? It's a sick world, and I'm just living in it.

I looked at my reflection, and for a moment I forgot I wasn't her. Then my eyes wandered down to the rusty edges of the mirror, the growing pile of dirty laundry near the foot of my bed, the double-wide litter box I hadn't cleaned in a week. Glamour!

I quickly packed a suitcase, tossing in a few backup wigs and some sunscreen. I looked at the time and temporarily panicked when I realized I'd miss that night's *Sex Island* episode. I'd been devoted to this show for weeks, developing what some might call a dependency. Now Luella was actually going to *Sex Island!* I hugged the cats as much as they would tolerate and headed to JFK, my head spinning.

I'll skip the gruesome details but I'll sum it up by saying the two words you never want to hear when it comes to air travel: *tiny plane.* Three long hours later, I landed on the island frazzled and ecstatic to be back on land.

It was almost 1 a.m. when I arrived. Even inside the airport, the air was warm and muggy. Everything smelled like salt water. I started to doubt whether my wigs would hold up in this weather. A short man and a tall woman greeted me at arrivals.

They revealed themselves to be the producers I spoke to over the phone. The short one was John Murphy, a nervous man in his mid-thirties with a receding hairline and blue eyes I didn't quite trust. He tried to smile.

"Welcome to the island! How was your flight?" he asked.

"A little rough," I said.

"Good, sounds good. Well, welcome to the island!" He gave me three consecutive pats on the shoulder. One of us was having a nervous breakdown, but I couldn't tell who.

The tall one, Stephanie Hillson, was a striking brunette in her early forties. I noticed she wore a large diamond ring on her left hand. Her nails were perfectly manicured with light pink polish — a color I exclusively associated with suburban moms and cotton candy. I looked down to see she was wearing the same stupid four-inch heels as me. At 1 a.m. In an airport. *Why do we do this to ourselves?* I was about to say, but she was already on her phone. We made our way to the arrivals parking lot.

John got in the driver's seat of a 12-seat passenger van and Stephanie sat shotgun, which I sort of took personally. I sat in the row directly behind them, even though I had my choice of nine other seats in the vehicle. I hoped it conveyed I was committed to the cause. School bus politics from twenty years ago were still fresh in my mind.

We made small talk on the ride over to the *Sex Island* compound. Over the years, I've gotten better at talking with the Luella teeth in, but I still have trouble with certain letters. All in all, I try not to speak as Luella more than is necessary. People assume Luella is standoffish or sensitive or even flirty — their interpretations run the whole gamut. But if there's one thing I've learned masquerading as a minimally-speaking hot woman, it's the less you talk, the more they do.

"How was your flight?" John asked for maybe the eighth time. His brain must've been elsewhere.

"A little rough," I repeated.

"You know, we really appreciate you coming out here," Stephanie chimed in. "If you don't mind, we have a Non-Disclosure Agreement we'd like for you to sign right away."

"Sure thing," I said.

Stephanie passed back a clipboard, and I carefully initialed *LVH* as the van bumped along the road. We eventually pulled into a parking lot in front of a sprawling one-story building. Only a few lights were still on, but it was very late. Most people had probably gone home for the night.

They led me inside. The hallways had wall-to-wall beige carpeting, and the building smelled like it'd just been cleaned by that pink stuff they use in elementary schools after some kid pukes in the gym. We walked past an older woman vacuuming as they led me into a room with five metal folding chairs and no table.

Stephanie offered me a chair, then sat down across from me. She looked nervous. "Luella, you don't need anything, do you? Water or coffee?"

"No, thanks," I said.

"Well, I'll tell you what we know," she proceeded. "We already spoke to your secretary — did she happen to fill you in?"

"A little," I said. If there were a camera, I would've winked at it.

"One of the show's contestants, David G, has been missing for two days, but of course, we're still optimistic," she said.

I nodded. The briefest of silences followed. John remained standing in the doorway.

"We've heard about your work and thought you might be able to find him," he said. "The island is fairly small, and the cast and crew all live within a couple of designated buildings, so it should be a fairly simple task. We just want you to work fast. Ideally, you find David G, he's alive, and his family and friends back home are none the wiser. Do you watch the show?"

I nodded. "I've seen it."

"Then you'll know David G was very well-liked among the cast and crew," Stephanie added.

"Any unknown visitors?" I asked.

"Never," Stephanie answered quickly. "Which is why your presence here may raise some red flags. So, we're proposing that you... John, how do I put this?"

"We're proposing that you join the cast," John said.

I was struggling to contain my combo-plate reaction of shock/excitement/about-to-barf. *Hope the cleaners have more of that pink stuff*, I thought.

"Oh?" I asked as nonchalantly as I could.

John continued, "We've given this a lot of thought. We often bring in wild card cast members to shake things up, and this will be the only way you'll have total access to the cast and crew without raising suspicion. I'm sure you're well-known within your profession, but to the general public, we think you'll come across like any other contestant on this show. I hope you don't mind me asking, but how old are you?"

Instead of answering, I opted to stare at him silently. He got the message and moved right along.

"As this is a very sensitive situation, we didn't want to tell you over the phone. We hope you'll understand and accept. Of course, you'll be compensated well. And no one will know who you truly are except for Stephanie and me. And presumably, your secretary." John handed me the contract as smoothly as he could muster. Was he trembling?

I glanced down at the figure at the bottom and did a double take. This would be, by far, my biggest case to date. I quickly signed the contract.

They loaded me down with a box of HR files on the cast and crew and took me to an apartment building across the lot. We rode the elevator up to the seventh floor. Stephanie handed me a key fob with 7E neatly written on it in white marker, while John went on and on about the building's cutting-edge security system. John and Stephanie each thanked me profusely for coming out on such short notice.

"Get some rest, because tomorrow's your first on-camera day," John added, giving me a double thumbs up. Oh boy.

I swiped the key fob and walked into my temporary apartment. It was minimally furnished and clean enough. There was a kitchenette with a few cooking supplies. In the bedroom, there was a queen-sized bed with a black and white patterned comforter. Based on a few faint but large stains, I gathered this thing was covered in all kinds of dried bodily fluids, so I gingerly scooted it off the bed and onto the ground. In the living room, there was a couch, a chair, and a small flat screen TV. The remote control was wrapped in plastic. T'was a real hygienic operation they were running.

I checked the time — it was already 2:30 a.m. I got undressed, unpacked my things and brushed my wigs. Sometimes when I'm away from home, I worry that I treat the wigs like my cats, but honestly, who could blame me. They kinda looked like long, blonde cats if you squinted hard enough and pretended cats didn't have faces. I popped out my fake teeth and scrubbed the makeup off my face. De-Luellafying after a long day always felt incredible.

I checked my messages. Only one, from Sophie.

Your cats stink

Just her charming way of saying she was taking care of them. What a freakin' doll.

I got out my reading glasses and brought the box of files into bed with me. There were profiles on each of the cast members. Most of the information I already knew from watching the hour-long show every night. I perused the background checks for a few of the crew members. There were some misdemeanors here and there but nothing out of the ordinary. Next I looked at David G's profile.

He'd been a college swimmer while getting his nursing degree from Penn State. He was born in Philadelphia. He loved The Roots. His last relationship was with a woman named Chloe, which ended once he was cast on the show. Why would a nurse in a stable relationship go on a reality sex show? Maybe this Chloe had some involvement in his disappearance. I paged through a few more crew profiles and paused when I found John's. He was also from Philadelphia. I perused his resumé. Up until now he'd only worked on true crime shows: *Murder on the Stairs*, *A Husband's Poison*, *The Angry Uncle*. I'd seen a few of these, and I could attest, they were bleak. How did he end up being a producer on *Sex Island*? Apparently this was John's first season, and a missing cast member probably didn't bode well. I made a mental note to watch John closely.

My eyes were closing, so I shut the box of files and turned off the light. My body was exhausted but my mind kept racing. I lay there studying the cracks in the popcorn ceiling until 4 a.m.

What felt like a minute later, I woke up to the sound of aggressive knocking. I looked at the clock — it was somehow already 6 in the morning.

WEDNESDAY

"Ms. Van Horn?" someone bellowed from the other side of the door.

I jumped out of bed and tried my very best to remember where the hell I was.

"Just a minute!" I yelled.

I scrambled around the small apartment trying to locate my wig and Luella teeth. I must've tripped over my own suitcase a dozen times. Out of breath and half put-together, I finally answered the door to a perky 20-something holding a clipboard, the accessory you never, ever want to see first thing in the morning. She had long red hair she'd braided and wrapped around her head a couple times for good measure. Her youthful face was covered in freckles, most likely a side effect of working long hours on a sunny island. She chewed a wad of gum that looked to be about three sticks worth.

"Good morning, Ms. Van Horn! I'm Isa, the first team's production assistant, which means I'll be your main contact here. Welcome to *Sex Island*! Time to get you into hair and makeup."

Oh no. I'd forgotten about hair and makeup. I stared at the alert creature before me, knowing whatever I said next could make or break both my investigation and my secret identity. I was already undercover as Luella, and now I was somehow supposed to go double-undercover as a "random *Sex Island* contestant." I was trying here, but I'm no Cindy freaking Sherman.

"I do my own. Part of my contract," I said.

Isa seemed to believe it, or maybe she just didn't want any extra hassle today. Either way, I had avoided Luella's first obstacle. Her second obstacle? Find out who wanted David G gone and why.

2

I followed Isa out of the apartment building and was shocked by how nice it was outside. The sun had just come up, and the breeze blowing off the ocean was cool. It felt discordant that David G could disappear in a place like this, a real-life Eden. We walked through the parking lot, much busier than it was late last night, abuzz with moving passenger vans and supply trucks. Wires the size of anacondas were taped to the ground, running through the entire lot like arteries. This had to be the home base for the *Sex Island* crew. I asked Isa where we were going, and she told me we were heading to my *honey wagon.*

"My *what?!*" I asked.

Isa only laughed and kept walking.

Eventually, Isa brought me to a small trailer, the so-called "honey wagon," and gestured to the stringy thing hanging on the back of the chair.

"That's your costume for today," she said, popping her gum.

"What?"

She pointed again to the thing on the chair. "That's your swim-suit. It's a beach day."

I shook my head. "Oh no. No."

Pivoting the conversation, Isa asked if I wanted any breakfast.

I tried to hold in a yawn. "Like what?"

"They can make you anything. The other women usually get egg-whites. You want that?"

"No."

"No, you don't want any breakfast?" Isa asked.

"No egg-whites. Get me whatever you get."

Isa looked around like she had about ten other things to do right now besides have this conversation. "I usually get egg-whites," she said.

"Okay. Egg-whites then."

I had a strong feeling I was going to hate being on TV.

Isa left me alone to figure out what to do with the thing on the back of the chair. There were strings and hooks and what looked like a button? I figured maybe this was one of those situations where I had to look at it from a distance for it to make sense. I stepped back as far as the trailer would allow (it turned out, two feet) and examined the "garment" from this new perspective.

I could sort of make out the parts that were supposed to cover my parts. It seemed less like a swimsuit and more like a legal loophole to be able to expose yourself in public. I took a deep breath, reminded myself David G was still missing, and tried putting it on. Twenty-five minutes of grunting and string-tying later, I was "wearing" it. I looked like I'd gotten caught naked in a ropes course.

The *honey wagon* left much to be desired, though it did have one of those lighted vanity mirrors. Turns out, they're real! There was a large plastic bowl on the dressing table containing a seashell and a single box of raisins. Hollywood really rolled out the red carpet for old Luella. Next to the bowl was a call sheet. I looked it over. It was surreal to be reading the printed names of the people I'd been watching have sex every night on TV. I scanned for David G's name. His call time said *TBD*.

The trailer's bathroom had one of those accordion doors that refused to close, and it took me ten minutes to figure out how to flush the toilet. Things were going well for me.

Sometime later, a PA who was not Isa dropped off a white blob in a take-out container, and I took this to be the egg-whites. I removed my Luella teeth and ate them quickly, as they tasted approximately like diet rubber.

The one thing Luella can never do is eat in front of people. Drinking is okay, but in my experience, eating with the prosthetic teeth opens up a whole can of worms. Unless its soup, the teeth will pop out when I least want them to, and I can't actually chew with them in, so it leads to a lot of minor choking. And I've found that minor choking tends to detract from the whole mysterious allure I'm going for here. Hence, I stand alone shoveling egg-whites into my mouth as fast as I can.

There was another loud rap at the door, and I assumed it was Isa this time, maybe with a second white blob for good sportsmanship.

"One second!" I quickly popped the Luella teeth back in and grabbed a bathrobe. I swung open the trailer door.

Standing before me was, no joke, the most gorgeous man I'd ever seen in my life. He was tan and ripped with perfect blonde, wavy, boy hair. He had chocolate brown eyes and long lashes that made him seem almost pretty. He wore red swim trunks, a tank top the color of cooked salmon, and what looked to be Prada flip-flops. I think I drooled a little looking at his arm muscles. He smiled at me, and it brightened his whole face. After what felt like four hundred minutes of ogling, I placed him. This was a *Sex Island* cast member!

"Hey, you're the new girl, right? I'm Phil. Welcome to the show!"

Yes! Phil from Wisconsin! The exercise guy!

"Hi," I said, quickly running my tongue along the front of my Luella teeth. Nice and secure.

Phil leaned casually against the trailer's door frame. "So, where'd you come from?"

"New York," I said.

"Nice. Statue of Liberty, right? Killer statue."

I nodded. Did he just say "killer statue"?

Phil kept on talking, as if the statue line was normal and good.

"Well, I just wanted to stop by and introduce myself. This place is kinda weird at first so if you have any questions, let me know. I'll be around." He paused and looked at me. "You okay?"

My face felt hot, and my hands felt sweatier than they'd ever been. "Oh yeah, fine!"

He laughed. "You're kinda funny!" With that, Phil hugged me. He did that thing where his arms went around my hips instead of my shoulders. In my 29 years on earth, I had learned there were friendly hugs and there were more-than-friendly hugs, and this was certainly a more-than-friendly hug. Phil smelled like coconut oil and sunshine. His arms felt broad and warm and— crap, now I was turned on.

He turned to go, then looked back with a little smile that brought out a single left dimple. Mmmph.

"Don't worry! You'll be fine," he said. "A word of advice: the egg-whites are bullshit. Next time, go with the protein waffles. See you on set."

I smiled back at him, a goofy, egg-white-eating grin. I was swooning, and I had never swooned in my adult life. Phil was easily the handsomest man I'd ever spoken to... and that hug. That hug! It felt like the kind of hug that would be illegal in 1903. It finally hit me — Luella was actually going to be on a reality show where the sole purpose was to have sex on television. This was the stupidest thing I'd ever done. I was here for David G. I was here for David G. I was here for David G.

3

What felt like twenty hours later, Isa was back at my trailer door. I looked at the clock — it was now 8 a.m.

"Ms. Van Horn, we'd like to invite you to set."

I swear I felt my stomach go out my rectum.

I followed Isa as she weaved us in and out of a throng of busy crew people. I felt self-conscious being nearly naked and kept hovering my hands over the bottom half of my body. I had one hand in front and one in back, like I was going for an Adam and Eve fig leaf sort of thing. It's not that I wasn't okay with my body the way it was. Sure, I've got a belly and my ass has gotten flatter and wider every day since I turned 27, but I was fine with all that. Because until now, I never had to be practically naked on camera next to 20-year-old reality TV stars. This experience was already a major turning point in my self-esteem.

Everyone on the crew seemed to be doing something important — hanging lights, carrying ladders, wearing actual clothes. Even drinking a coffee seemed to be an activity of significance around here. Adjacent to the parking lot where they kept the trailers and gear trucks was a stunning white sand beach. I must've missed it in the darkness the night before. I followed as Isa made a right turn, and suddenly there was sand beneath me. It was soft, powdery, and the color of tapioca pudding.

Once we were on the beach, I got my first good look at the ocean. The blue of the water made me gasp. The color was cartoonishly vibrant, as if it were drawn in magic marker. Isa was seemingly over the whole beautiful vista thing. She looked at her watch and sighed.

"You can go see the water if you're quick about it. Two minutes tops."

I made my way down to the shore. The water was so clear there, I could see little fish and shells and individual grains of sand. The waves were gentle, making swooshing sounds that were nearly hypnotic. And, I kid you not, the palm trees were swaying in the breeze. I'll stop.

Two minutes on the dot later, Isa wrangled me back, leading me to a large beach hut covered in tropical flowers. As we got closer, I recognized Phil and waved to him. He waved back and I blushed. Absolutely humiliating. I felt like an eighth grader.

Phil was standing with a few other cast members I recognized as Tasha, Sarah, David N, Nate, Ethan, and Blair. Ooh, I loved Blair. She could be so mean. One time she stuck a wad of chewed gum in Sarah's long, blonde hair because she "couldn't find a trash can." In a confessional, she once told millions of viewers that Nate's balls "smelled like Lipton's soup mix." She had curly brown hair, a flat stomach, and I'll say it, breasts the size of cantaloupes. It's possible Blair was made in a lab for reality TV.

As I approached the group, Isa made introductions.

"Hey folks, this is Luella, she's going to be joining us as the wild card."

Me, the wild card!

"Hi." I tried hard to swallow anything that could be construed as fangirl energy.

The collective group murmured some casual hellos. Nate even flashed me a peace sign. For them, I gathered this was just a typical Wednesday.

They all looked so different in person. David N wasn't nearly as skinny, and I noticed for the first time he had bright green eyes. On television, Ethan looked practically orange, but here he just looked like a guy who got his money's worth in the tanning booth. I could see Sarah's individual toe rings... I counted seven!

Isa got a far-off look as someone spoke into her earpiece.

"All right, in a few minutes Luella's going to be coming in through the Hibiscus Arch camera left. I need jealous reactions from Sarah and Blair and a sexy reaction from Nate."

I tried to remind myself this was somehow detective work.

Phil spoke up. "Hey Isa? I'd like to do a sexy reaction, too."

Nate let out an exasperated whine. "Why can't I be the only sexy one for once?!"

Isa held up her finger waiting for the person in the earpiece to respond.

"Okay, we're gonna have both Nate and Phil giving sexy reactions."

Nate sulked.

Isa continued, "Ethan and David N, let's have you wrestling in the background. And Tasha, we just want you to stand there."

Tasha crossed her arms and looked toward the ocean, her long black hair shining in the sun. "No, bitch," she said under her breath.

For what it's worth, Tasha did technically just stand there. I was *amongst professionals.*

I was escorted to the *Hibiscus Arch camera left.* Isa got that far-off look again as someone in her earpiece gave her further instructions. A sound guy came over to give me a microphone pack on a lanyard. As he placed it around my neck, he muttered, "Just don't touch it, and you'll be good." I'd once heard that same sentence from my 85-year-old male gynecologist.

Isa addressed me. "Luella, you're going to walk through the Hibiscus Arch, shake your hair, and give a smoldering look to camera. This footage will be in slow-motion, so try not to blink at all. And stop covering your body — that's why you're here. Ready in 4, 3, 2... Action!"

And just like that, Isa was gone, and I was left to smolder and not blink and be practically naked on national television.

I decided to just focus on the not blinking. I looked at Phil, who was looking back at me in a way I can only describe as *we're having sex right now.* I had been married for six years and had never been looked at like that before. I tried to remember this was for television, that there were hot lights everywhere, and cameras, and I was here to find a missing man, and if all that weren't enough, this wasn't even me. Phil was staring at Luella van Horn. But I still couldn't get enough of that look.

Which was great, because we did that same thing fourteen times. Fourteen times I walked through the Hibiscus Arch, and fourteen times he stared at me like I was a Christmas ham. But the thing is, I kind of loved being the Christmas ham. I started to understand why all these people did was have sex and scream at each other. A makeup artist came up to me between takes eleven and twelve. She introduced herself as Hannah.

"Honey, I know you do your own makeup but you're sweating like a pig. Okay if I give you a little dab?"

"Oh! Sure," I said. Pig. Pig becoming ham.

After that fourteenth take, Isa came back and announced that they got what they needed and we could all take a break. I decided I had done enough acting for one day. It was time to do my real job and find David G. Before I could re-orient myself toward the parking lot, I found Phil standing right in front of me.

"Hey, great work out there. I think we have something going, yeah?" He shifted his weight from one Prada flip-flop to the other.

I looked at him for a second trying to see if he was serious. "Now *you're* kinda funny."

He raised his eyebrows at me. "I'm serious! You're cute."

"Uh, I gotta go do... something." And with that excellent line, I ran away on the sand in heels, which, in itself, is a huge accomplishment.

I needed to talk to someone — anyone — who didn't want to have immediate televised sex with me. I found a snack table and decided to linger there for a minute to get my bearings. Surely the cast and crew might say things there that they might not near the cameras. The topic of David G could come up. I made myself a coffee with cream and five sugars and drank it slowly.

John Murphy, the short producer with the blue eyes, sidled up to me. It looked like he hadn't slept much the night before. This morning, he was wearing a bright blue Hawaiian shirt that felt a little on the nose for a *Sex Island* producer.

"Hey, sorry for all the takes. We just needed to establish your character. Now you can mostly go about your business here."

"But I was only on camera for ten minutes," I said.

"Oh, don't worry. A reality TV editor can magically make an hour of television with, like, twenty minutes of raw footage and forty minutes of recaps. How's the investigation going? Any leads?"

John chewed on his thumb. From the looks of it, he'd been chewing on his thumb for the last three days. I took another sip of the too-sweet coffee.

"Not yet," I said.

"Well, we really appreciate you being here — being on camera, all of it. So, you think you could wrap this up in the next day or two? We're kind of on a time crunch, I'm sure you understand."

"I understand." Next day or two? Was he serious? To no one's surprise, John's thumb started bleeding. He sucked on it and continued talking, now in a low whisper.

"It's been three days now that he's been missing, and I know, I know... we should've notified his family. But you understand, right? They'd leak it to the press, and then the network would get upset and we'd all get canned. For some of us, it's our first season. And it could still turn out to be a lot of hullaballoo for nothing." He grabbed a powdered donut and ate it so fast, I thought he'd form a cloud.

"Who saw him last?" I asked.

"Well, it's Wednesday now, and he didn't show up to set on Monday. Something could've happened over the weekend — Saturday and Sunday are the cast and crew's days off. If and when bad things happen, it's usually on a weekend. I think Tasha was the last one to see him late Friday night. They were together. Are. Are together."

So, when John told me on the phone that David G had been gone for only 48 hours, he was omitting the weekend, just counting Monday and Tuesday. Very strange.

"Um, to answer your question, Tasha was probably the last one to see him," he continued, digging through the mixed nuts for a cashew. He popped it into his mouth and chewed fast.

If something happened to David G on Saturday or Sunday, by now he'd either be in horrible shape or dead. I didn't have high hopes. I was no veteran detective, but I'd done this long enough to know that something bad had probably happened. Judging by the airport alone, the island wasn't large. Looking around, I started to wonder how long a dead body could go without being noticed around here.

John took my silence as a reason to excuse himself. "Well, I'll leave you to it. Let me know if you have any questions. Just F.Y.I., some of the crew can be a little shifty. Pretty much the whole grip department has a criminal record, so I'd keep an eye on them."

John walked away, glancing back at me only four times before he realized it was getting weird. I looked around at the bustling cast and crew. Could there be a dark underbelly to this place? The sky was blue, the water was clear, and everywhere, young people were chatting, working, laughing. Then I saw someone staring at me from behind the Hibiscus Arch. They ducked back, but I spied their long, straight, black hair. It had to be Tasha. I wondered how long she'd been watching me and why.

4

Tasha was a 22-year-old fitness instructor from Orange County, California. In addition to her signature long, black hair, she was known for her 24K diamond bellybutton ring and her big, brown doe eyes. One time in an interview with E! News, she told the reporter she hated "the smell of air." Tasha was well-known for her shocking and unfiltered contributions to the show. In one famous confessional, she claimed, "In an ideal world I would have sex sixteen times a day." That pretty much sealed her fate as a regular from then on.

Most recently on the show, she'd been paired David G, but before that she'd had flings with Nate and this other guy named Noah who got voted off two weeks in for being openly "afraid of cunnilingus." Rumor had it, he was getting his own spin-off show where he reviewed restaurants, called *Noah's Eating Out*. It really begged the question: what is life?

Most episodes, Tasha came across as irritable, jealous, and entitled. As a viewer, I didn't like her. But the show was so hyper edited, it was hard to know what everyone was actually like. David G's absence was raising suspicion amongst the show's die-hard fans on online forums. Many were quick to blame Tasha, and a meme had been going around saying she had the "breasts of a killer," whatever that meant. Sometimes misogyny can be so creative.

Tasha knew I'd seen her behind the Hibiscus Arch, and maybe for that reason, she was walking toward me now. I felt a chill run down my spine. Maybe it was because a murderer was approaching, maybe it was because I was wearing practically no clothes at all and there was a slight breeze. I couldn't say. She approached the snack table without acknowledging me, so I pretended to stare straight ahead. From my periphery, I watched her pick up a turkey sandwich, remove and eat the turkey, then place the bread back on the tray. She was now my number one suspect.

I wanted her to talk to me, so I picked up a sandwich from the tray, fished out the lettuce, then put the sandwich back, hoping game would recognize game. I put a small piece of the lettuce in my mouth and attempted to swallow it whole like a pill. Any chewing was out of the question. Finally, she mumbled something. I turned to her.

"Ditch your mic pack and follow me," she mumbled again. This time I heard her.

She walked toward the parking lot. I tucked my mic pack into the dirt of a potted palm tree and followed her. I saw Isa take notice and say something into her walkie-talkie. Were PAs always supposed to be watching, or was Isa especially diligent? I planned to read Isa's file when I got home that night.

I followed as Tasha zigzagged her way through the lot, then onto a side street populated by a few small businesses. We passed a handful of locals doing their errands. There was a newsstand, a laundromat, and a small credit union that looked liked it'd been closed for many years. The street curved and eventually dead-ended with a little cafe. I had a feeling we weren't supposed to journey this far during our break, and I wondered if the locals were used to two American women in bikinis and high heels wandering about their town.

Tasha sat down at a table and tossed me a well-worn laminated menu. I took the seat across from her. As luck would have it, my menu was covered in large orange stains. How appetizing!

A waiter came by to take our orders. Tasha smiled and pointed at two pictures, one of a latte and one of a plate of fried plantains. I smiled too, and pointed to a picture of a glass of tropical fruit juice. The waiter chuckled, jotted down the orders, and walked away. Our interaction left me unsettled.

Tasha waited until the waiter was out of earshot. "You know you ordered a double daiquiri? New girl, it's not even 11 a.m."

"Oh no," I said.

"Don't worry, I'll split it with you. Unless you really need a double, and if that's the case, I get it."

"I don't," I insisted.

"You don't say much, do you?"

I laughed, not knowing what else to do. Already, Tasha seemed more grounded than the woman I knew from TV.

"Look, I know you're new, so I just wanted to let you know what you're getting into here. I'm sure you've heard about David G, right?"

I gave her a small nod, hoping she'd interpret that as a *go on*.

"Well, he is, like, nowhere to be found and, like, nobody even cares. We're just being told to go on with the show like it's normal. So, okay, we're bringing in new cast members now? No offense, but what the hell?"

"Nobody's seen him?" I asked. John said Tasha was the last person to see him Friday evening. I wondered if she'd confirm that timeline.

Before I could get into it, Tasha shushed me as the waiter came by with our drinks. Mine was served with two umbrellas and a generous slice of pineapple. Tasha was quiet until the waiter disappeared back into the kitchen. She leaned closer to me.

"So, don't tell anyone this. I saw him on Saturday but I think Nate saw him after me. David G told me he was going to hang out with Nate that weekend. They're, like, best friends. But then by Monday David G had completely disappeared, and Nate claimed he never saw him. Also, just F.Y.I., we're technically not allowed to be outside the compound, and we could get in a lot of trouble if anyone caught us here. You more than me, 'cause you're new."

I nodded. Tasha took my drink and gulped down a quarter of it.

"Whoa, that's yummy. You should try it," she said, already beginning to hiccup.

I took a sip. It tasted like a rum-flavored slushy. Seconds later, I got the hiccups, too. Tasha and I made for quite the pair.

She held her latte in both hands and blew on it, temporarily distracted by the jiggling foam. "Like, I don't even know why I'm telling you this, I just don't know what the hell else to do."

"Are you and David G still together?" I asked.

"Well, we broke up on Friday, then on Saturday, we met up to process the break up. He wanted to get back together, but I said we should feel it out. He wasn't acting like himself. He didn't even want to have sex with me anymore, said he "didn't feel up to it." I thought maybe he was seeing someone else. Maybe Sarah? She sucks, though."

I mean, Tasha wasn't wrong. As a viewer I could confirm: Sarah did kind of suck. She was nice, and there's just no place for that kind of behavior on *Sex Island*. Thirty percent of her OnlyFans proceeds went to a local food pantry. Ridiculous.

The waiter arrived with the plate of fried plantains. My stomach rumbled. I ran my tongue over the fake Luella teeth to remind myself to not even try it. Tasha fanned the plate. I noticed she was missing one of her red acrylic nails. The right hand thumb. I wondered where that ended up.

Tasha groaned. "Ugh, they make everything so hot here. It's really annoying when you're trying to eat fast. Can't they cook them without getting them so damn hot?" She glanced up at the clock on the wall. "We gotta head back soon, or they'll start to notice."

I tried to steer her back on track. "What time on Saturday?"

"Okay, are you a detective or something?"

"No!" I said, taking another sip of the daiquiri.

"Well, I don't know, maybe 11 at night?"

She picked up a fat plantain with her fingers, took a small bite, and dropped it directly onto the table. "Ugh, it's still too hot!"

Then I heard someone shout, "Tasha!" We both turned to see Isa running into the cafe. She was out of breath and held her clipboard under her arm.

"You guys can't leave set. Tasha, we've talked about this. Let's go!"

My mind was racing. I understood there was a rule, but exactly *why* couldn't we leave set? And how did Isa find us? Was it normal for a PA to know exactly where each cast member was at all times? If so, maybe Isa knew something about David G's disappearance.

Tasha groaned, fished a wilted $50 dollar bill out of her bikini top, tossed it on the table and followed Isa out. I followed them, hiccuping, and wondering why Tasha told me what she told me, and if it was anywhere near the truth.

5

Once we were back on the lot, I tried retracing my early morning steps to get back to the apartment building. The afternoon sun was becoming oppressive. I now understood why we started filming so early in the morning. I felt beads of sweat rolling down my back. I was hungry and agitated. I hadn't slept enough, and I needed to organize my thoughts. I needed to eat. Most importantly, I needed to put on some clothes.

After a few wrong turns, I finally found the apartment building. On the elevator ride up I started fantasizing about hot dogs, ice cream, lobster rolls. How does one eat meals around here, I wondered. The elevator dinged for the seventh floor, and I got off, day-dreaming of the fast-food chain, Sonic. Would they have Sonic on the island? I walked down the hallway to my apartment and noticed my door was left slightly ajar. Sonic was no longer top of mind.

I felt immediately on edge, but maybe I'd forgotten to close the door in the early morning rush. I walked in hesitantly. Normally I carry pepper spray, but there was nowhere to hide it on a string bikini. The place smelled differently than before. There was a new musk, possibly sweat. Or sweat mixed something worse; rotting vegetables, ferret. Someone was still in there or had just left moments ago. Best case scenario, this was some kind of new cast member hazing ritual.

Worst case, I was about to be dead. Either way, the intruder had seen my wigs.

The apartment layout was simple enough. Upon entry there was a kitchenette, which was separated from the living room by a breakfast bar with two stools. The bedroom was to the right of the living room, through a doorway. The bathroom was attached to the bedroom.

From where I stood frozen at the front door, I could see all of the living room and kitchenette. But the bedroom door was closed and that made my heart drop into my stomach. I removed my heels. As quietly as possible, I tiptoed through the living room to the closed bedroom door. I listened for movement of any kind, but I could only hear the blood rushing past my ears. My mouth was so dry I couldn't swallow. I needed to stabilize. I needed this moment to be over.

In dealing with a possible intruder situation, there are two schools of thought. One is to go fast and the other is to go slow. As I stood facing the closed bedroom door, I considered both options. Open it slowly, then whoever was behind there had ample time to see and kill me. Open it quickly, then whoever was behind there got so startled that they killed me. I opted for fast. I swung open the door and quickly scanned the bedroom. Not a soul was there. I looked under the bed, no one. I ripped open the closet, nobody. A wave of relief poured over me, until I realized the bathroom door was also shut. Shit.

At least now I had a system. Do it fast. If anyone was still in that apartment with me, they were behind that bathroom door. And if they were planning to off me, I'd given them plenty of time to prepare. I took a deep breath, maybe the first one I'd taken since I'd gotten inside the apartment. I yanked open the bathroom door and jumped to stay behind it as it swung. I paused. There was no sound coming from the other side. I peered around the flimsy plywood (some protection that would have been) and to my shock, there was no one there. Just the lemon yellow tiles. The toilet. The sink. My mind started to do mental gymnastics — maybe I *had* closed these doors but left the front one open. It was entirely possible... But the ferret smell was stronger in here. Much stronger.

Then I noticed the bathtub. The shower curtain had been pulled closed, but there was something in the tub. From this angle I could see a swath of dark denim peaking through the water-stained plastic curtain. I stepped closer, opened the curtain, and looked down. A wave of the stench hit me. There was David G, dead in my bathtub.

6

It took me a few seconds to get my bearings. It'd been a short-lived relief encountering no live intruders. But someone had been in my apartment during the six hours I'd been gone and dropped a dead body in my bathtub. From the looks of it, he'd been dead for quite a while. The timing of it all made me wonder if Tasha's off-compound outing was a planned distraction. Anyway, someone out there wanted me to know David G had been murdered.

I knelt down to get a closer look. I would have put money on the fact that he'd been dead for at least 24 hours, maybe more. I'd been teaching myself forensic science with books from the library and embarrassingly, old episodes of *Forensics Files*. In the 24-72 hour window, the internal organs decomposed and the body began to smell. He was definitely ripe. I touched his arm, and it was no longer stiff. Rigor mortis had subsided. Another sign it might've been more than 24 hours.

David G's hair was disheveled. His skin looked pale, almost gray, but he was fully dressed, in dark jeans and a white T-shirt that was somehow spotless. Somebody must have redressed him at some point. From where I was kneeling, I could see there was some skin discoloration on the back of his neck. His blood had likely pooled there before relocating to my bathtub, which meant he must've been lying down at the prior location. I imagined his back was discolored, too. With his T-shirt on, I couldn't be sure, and I was hesitant to move his body too much before the police arrived.

I scanned for any obvious cause of death. There were no wounds, no blood, no random bruises, no signs of asphyxia. Maybe an overdose. Poison was possible. I noticed a strange, circular cut under his navel, but it didn't seem to be a fatal wound. I looked at his face. His eyes were open, but they were glassy and dry. I kept thinking how young he looked, but I needed to keep my emotions at bay. At that moment, it was imperative I operate with a scientific brain. If I let myself feel what I really felt, I'd be inconsolable.

I took some photos with my phone, then went to sit on the toilet to type out some notes and nearly fell in. Whoever had been in here had left the seat up. How did I not notice this before? I called John.

He answered out of breath. "I'm on the elliptical, what's up?"

"I found David G," I said.

"What? Where?"

"My bathtub."

"You're joking," he said. I heard beeping, then the whoosh-whoosh of the elliptical machine stopped.

"Looks like murder," I said.

"Don't call the police. I'll be right there."

In general, I answer to the check-signers, but it felt wrong not involving the authorities at this point. David G wasn't coming back to life anytime soon. I called Stephanie and told her the same thing I'd told John.

"Does John know?" she asked. It was her first and only question.

"Yes," I said.

"I'll be there soon."

I figured I had about ten minutes to grab a robe and put away any of my belongings that screamed *double identity* before anyone got there. I was never one to futz with a crime scene, but I wasn't trying to out Luella as fictional, either. Apparently, I had misjudged the time because I heard a knock at the door about ninety seconds after I hung up with Stephanie.

I shoved the rest of my wigs in an empty suitcase, zipped it, and kicked it under the bed. I ran to open the door. John stood there, out of breath.

"You got here fast," I said.

"Well..." he heaved. "You know..."

I led him in, but John wouldn't go past the middle of the living room.

I gestured toward the bathroom. "He's in there."

John looked down. "Uh-huh. Did you... uh, call Stephanie? Is she coming? I should probably call Stephanie, right?" He took out his phone and began fiddling with it.

"On her way," I told him.

John paced the floor, then stopped. He looked up. "You called her?"

"Yeah."

"What'd she say?"

Just then, someone else knocked on the door. We both jumped.

John lowered his voice to a stage whisper. "Are you sure he's dead?"

"I'm sure."

"Shit! Stephanie's going to make this a whole thing!"

"It is… a whole thing," I said. Either John was guilty of something horrible or on very good drugs.

"No, I know, I know. I just don't think we need the police involved yet. It'll make everything a nightmare." He was pacing so fast, I thought he might forge a small road down the middle of the fake wooden floor.

"John, he's dead."

"Are you sure?" he asked.

"Yes."

"But why is he here in your room?! It's like, did someone know you were investigating his disappearance?"

"I don't know," I said.

"I didn't tell anyone, but maybe Stephanie did…" John said, biting into his raw thumb.

The more I talked with John, the more I felt like an accomplice to something I didn't want anything to do with. The knocking had become more insistent. John plopped down on the couch and put his head in his hands. I went to answer the door.

Stephanie stood in the doorway looking like hell. Truly, like a cat that got run over by a large truck and managed to live. In retrospect I should have left her there. Because the minute she entered the apartment, I think she lost her mind.

She brushed past me, only addressing John on the couch.

"What the hell is going on, John? Did you call the police?" If John was at an eight, Stephanie was at an eleven. John stood, waving his arms over his head and walking in a circle.

"I don't know what's going on! I just got here two minutes ago!" he screamed.

"Well, then call the police!" Stephanie's face was now a shade of red I'd categorize as *true beet*. I hadn't seen this side of her before.

"Are you sure?" John hissed. "Because once we do that, we are opening a huge can of worms, Stephanie!"

"Do you want to see him?" I asked.

"No!" they both yelled at the same time.

Only Stephanie followed me into the bedroom. In my haste to let John in, I'd accidentally closed the bathroom door, making this moment feel much more *dramatic reveal* than I'd intended. I glanced over at Stephanie, hoping she had a strong stomach.

I opened the bathroom door, and the ferret smell hit us again. Stephanie screamed. She staggered backward out of the small bathroom, then slowly made her way back in. Over and over she moaned, "No, no, no, no," as if that might bring him back.

Stephanie couldn't take her eyes off David G's face. I scanned the bathroom for any clues I'd missed earlier. And that's when I saw my tooth case. On the sink. Out in the open. Just to be clear, what I'm talking about is a small, red plastic case that says "Dental Prosthetics DO NOT EAT" on top in case someone very stupid mistakes it for a snack cake holder. I looked to Stephanie, hoping she was still focused on David G. Of course she was. I crossed over to the sink and palmed the case. And that's the moment Stephanie lost interest in the dead body.

"What's that you've got?" she asked.

"What?"

"What are you holding?"

I wracked my brain for something one could find in a bathroom. "Lube," I finally said.

"Oh," Stephanie replied, but I could tell she wasn't buying it. She shifted her focus back to David G's dead body. She peeled back the plastic shower curtain and took another good look. She put her hand over her mouth and sank down to her knees on the cold tile floor.

"I'm sorry," I said, studying her face. She looked devastated. She closed the curtain but stayed kneeling.

"John doesn't think we should call the police," she said in a very small voice. "What do you think we should do?"

"Call the police," I said.

"Yes. Yes, I think so, too. It's going to make producing this TV show a living hell, but David G is... oh God."

Stephanie took a deep inhale, stood, and left the bathroom. I shoved the tooth case into an empty drawer near the sink and joined her where she'd taken a seat on my bed. She'd pulled out her phone and started dialing the police when John walked in.

"Stephanie, what are you doing?" John looked sweaty and pale.

"I'm calling the police. We can't hide this."

"Stop! Hang up!" John was practically foaming at the mouth.

But it was too late. An operator had picked up.

"Hi, my name is Stephanie Hillson, I'm a producer with *Sex Island*. There's a dead body at 30 Beach Street, Apt. 7E."

John resumed his anxious pacing in my bedroom, which suddenly felt very small with three grown adults in it.

"Stephanie, are you listening to me?" John shouted.

Stephanie looked up at him angrily, holding her hand over the phone. "What!" she whispered.

"You're going to deal with this yourself. I'm out of here!" And with that, John stormed out of the apartment and slammed the door behind him.

Stephanie and I looked to each other. Why was John so afraid of the police seeing David G's dead body, when he couldn't even look at it himself? I tried to ask her about John, but she just sat there, softly weeping. I offered her a glass of water, which she took but didn't drink. The terrible part of me wondered whether her tears were genuine.

About thirty minutes later, the police came. The two lead detectives introduced themselves — a Detective Sandro and a Detective Johannes. Johannes had a mustache that would've made Tom Selleck jealous. He put us in the living room and told us to sit tight. Eventually he and Detective Sandro sat down and asked us some basic questions. "Do you know this man?" "When did you find him?" "How did you find him?" "Have you noticed anyone acting strangely today?" More police came. They took pictures and dusted for fingerprints. Ultimately, they bagged David G's body and wheeled him out on a stretcher. As they squeakily made their way down the hallway, I saw one door open just a little bit. All I could see inside was someone's long black hair.

7

After the detectives had left for the night, Stephanie suggested I relocate to an apartment on the fourth floor, seeing as my current place was considered an active crime scene. She kept insisting it was "for my safety." I figured if someone could break in and drop off a dead body on the seventh floor, they could probably do something just as horrible three floors below, but I didn't say anything. She stood watching me from the living room as I threw everything into two suitcases as fast as I could.

Stephanie gave me the key fob for my new apartment and told me to call her if there were any issues. She looked like she might collapse. When I asked if she was okay, she insisted she just needed some rest.

"Did you know David G before coming here?" she asked.

"I didn't," I said.

"It's just strange. You show up here, and a day later he turns up dead in your bathtub."

"What are you saying?" I asked.

"Sorry, I must be tired. Goodnight, Luella."

"'Night," I said, but she was already halfway down the hall.

The new place had the same layout as my old one, so I made myself at home pretty quickly. An hour later, I got a text from Isa:

Hi Luella, tomorrow's shoot is canceled. Enjoy your day!

Seeing as a cast member's dead body had just turned up, "enjoy" seemed like an odd verb choice. Isa certainly was a strange bird. That night, I didn't get much sleep and when I woke up the next morning, it was somehow already 9 a.m.

THURSDAY

I hadn't worked as Luella in a while, and my body felt sore from all the activity. I took a long shower in an untainted bathtub and ordered delivery from that cafe I'd gone to yesterday. A raspberry croissant, hash browns and a breakfast quesadilla. It arrived a half hour later, and I ate it all within ninety seconds.

John was obviously unhinged, but I couldn't stop thinking about Stephanie. Her reaction to seeing David G's body in the bathtub was so odd, to say the least. She was both distraught and removed. And our conversation from last night was haunting me. I drank a pot of coffee as I read up on her file.

Stephanie Hillson was recently divorced with two kids, both of them now tweenagers who lived with their dad back in LA. She'd worked as an executive producer of *Sex Island* for the last five seasons. Before that, she'd been a producer on a show called *Roamers*, which I sort of remembered being about guys who drove around trying to competitively pick up women. High quality stuff. Her birthday was November 2. I looked up her astrological sign for kicks — a Scorpio. Loyal, devoted, passionate. Sure, why not.

I got dressed and decided to pay Stephanie a visit, check in on her. I texted her, asking which room she was in. She responded right away: *7F.* So Stephanie lived on the seventh floor, just next door to my old place. Could she have heard someone or something going into my apartment yesterday?

In my opinion, everyone involved in this show was living way too close together. No wonder somebody got murdered. Maybe it was the Case of the Too Loud Stereo, or the Incense That Incensed... So Much Anger That Someone Killed Somebody Else. All right. Sorry, I know. Real dead guy. Not funny.

I put on the wig and the teeth, some red lipstick, and a short white knit dress I felt I couldn't really pull off, even as Luella. I took the elevator up to the seventh floor and walked down the hall to 7F. There it was, separated from my first apartment by what I assumed was a very thin wall. I knocked twice. Stephanie opened the door within seconds, looking scarily radiant. Her eyes were rimmed red, but she had her brown hair pulled back in a high ponytail, and she was wearing a blazer. On a Thursday morning. Inside her apartment. Very weird. She scanned the hallway and seeing that the coast was clear, she hurriedly invited me inside.

Her apartment had the same layout as both of mine, but she had little personal touches everywhere. Framed photos of her with her ex-husband and kids, a large tapestry on the wall, a blanket on the couch. A tea kettle whistle sounded.

"Tea?" she offered.

"Sure."

Stephanie poured hot water into a big yellow teapot.

"Is green okay?" She sniffled. "Cookie?"

Less than twelve hours ago we both saw a dead body, now she was offering me cookies? "You okay?" I asked her.

She was moving around like a hummingbird. A crying hummingbird.

"Huh? Oh fine! I'm glad you stopped by. I wanted to talk to you. Sit, sit!" She blew her nose into a tissue and threw it in the garbage. From where I was standing, I could see the can was nearly full of them.

I sat down on the couch next to a sequined throw pillow that said *Girl Boss*. Stephanie handed me one of the two steaming mugs. She sat beside me, quietly blowing on her tea and staring straight ahead.

"Stephanie?"

She quickly shook her head and looked at me. "Oh! I meant to tell you, you're doing really well on the show!"

"What?"

"Ratings wise. People love you. They think you have a lot of potential for sexual chaos."

That wasn't a sentence I'd forget anytime soon. I felt a renewed gratitude that my ex-husband hated reality TV. If he saw me like this, I think his head would fall off. Fall off and roll right out the door (our Staten Island house was unleveled).

"Well... thanks."

She took a sip of her tea, then carefully set her mug down on a coaster. It had one of those drawings of a 1950s woman on it, and it said, "I drink for your health!" I read it a couple times over before it started to make sense to me. Maybe I needed more coffee this morning.

She clapped her hands together and turned toward me. "Luella, I wanted to ask you. Are you planning to continue your investigation?"

"Yes?" I said.

"I only ask because I'm sure the local police are going to conduct their own investigation, independently."

"I'm going to continue," I said.

"Okay, well, do what you need to do, and let me know if we can be of any help!" She took another gulp of tea.

I nodded and took a sip. Lord almighty, it was hot. How was she drinking this?

"What's John's deal?" I asked.

At that, Stephanie shoved a shortbread cookie into her mouth. She seemed to swallow it whole like a snake would do to a small beaver.

"Oh, he's fine. Last night he wasn't acting normal."

"Yeah?" I asked, blowing on my tea.

"I only met him when we started working together a few months ago, and he doesn't tend to socialize outside of work. I'm sure, like everybody, he's got some skeletons in his closet." She smiled at me, then grabbed another tissue and blew her nose. I wondered what kind of skeletons.

Stephanie continued, "I think he and David G knew each other from way back." She paused. "Luella, do you think this was a suicide?" She searched my eyes for something between reassurance and corroboration.

"I don't," I said.

"Well, that's too bad," she said.

"That's too bad?" I asked.

"Oh! You know I didn't mean it like that." She waved her hand in front of her. "So, what will you do today... to investigate?"

"I was going to talk to the cast," I said.

"Where?" she asked, with what seemed like a tinge of passive-aggressiveness.

"Where do you suggest?"

"You don't know about Cantina?" she asked. I shook my head.

"Well, on days off, the cast mostly hangs out at this bar in town called Cantina. They're not supposed to leave campus, but keeping them all within the compound can be like herding cats. Anyway, you might learn something useful if you go."

I couldn't get a good read on Stephanie. Was she actually trying to help me? She'd clearly been crying, but lots of people cry for all kinds of messed up reasons. One time in the Port Authority bus station I saw a finance bro bawling his eyes out, and when I asked what the trouble was, he said he was just really tired and his tooth "kinda hurt." Anyway, I figured this was my cue to leave.

I stood and nodded to the mug. "Thanks for the tea."

"Oh, Luella, I realized with the rush, we didn't tell you some of the move-in basics. There's a pantry and group fridge on two, take whatever you want." She rummaged in her pocket and pulled out a key. "And here's your mailbox key. Your mailbox number will correspond to your original room, 7E."

"Copy that," I said.

I took the mailbox key, and she brought me in for a big hug.

"Take care of yourself, Luella."

What the hell did that mean? I left Stephanie's room feeling strange, like she didn't trust me at all. But why?

As I took the elevator down, I checked my phone. I had five messages, all from Sophie.

Your cats stink

mail is piling up

Why is mail for Luella van Horn coming to your house? She is on Sex Island!!!

Your friend????

I love her!!!! Why she friends w you?

For the record, Meatloaf and Meatball did not stink, and in fact, they both smelled incredible. But I was comforted knowing they were getting some company, even if it was from the grumpiest woman alive.

Weirdness with Stephanie aside, I did want to figure out the connection between John and David G. I intended to read up on John's file, see where it might overlap with David G's personal history. First, I wanted to check my mail. You never knew… Maybe whoever left David G in my bathtub also sent me a thank you note, or maybe there was some tie to whoever lived in 7E before me. I arrived on the first floor and eventually found my way to the mail room, a small area behind the elevators. I found 7E's mailbox and unlocked it.

Inside there was a grocery store coupon, an advertising mailer for a local sandwich shop, and a small black envelope. The envelope was made of a heavy-weight, high-quality paper, like a wedding invitation. I turned it over, and then my heart stopped. In block white print, the envelope was addressed to *Marie*. I looked around, and finding myself alone, I opened the envelope slowly.

Most people assume a random scary envelope might contain some kind of airborne horror powder, but for whatever reason I wasn't getting an Anthrax vibe. I got the sense that whoever sent this letter wanted me scared, but not dead. Why else would they address the note to Marie?

My blood ran cold thinking of all the people who could have sent it. Possibly the convicted murderer Taylor Bell. Or Mark Lassiter, the man I wrongfully sent to jail before I realized Taylor Bell was the bad guy. Maybe my ex-husband, if he'd had a few too many beers and got to digging around. I still wasn't sure how much he knew and didn't know about Luella. Nothing like an ominous letter to make me realize how many men out there wanted me living in fear.

Inside the envelope was a 3x5 inch black card. In neat, white writing, it said:

I know who you are. I can help.

Was this why Stephanie told me to check my mail? Did she send this to me? If so, why would she have hired me in the first place? Why the tea and cookies act? I got the feeling she thought I was the one who killed David G. Was this all some kind of trap?

There was no address on the envelope, just my name. Whoever sent this to me must've lived within the compound. Who here would know to call me Marie? Maybe this was all a mistake — maybe there was another person named Marie who lived in 7E just before me, who needed some anonymous person's help. Doubtful, but it was briefly comforting. I tried to put Taylor Bell out of my mind for now.

Just then, I heard someone coming. I shoved the letter into my purse and tried my best to look like I wasn't on the brink of a panic attack. I yanked on my mailbox key but it was stuck in the lock. I turned it to the left, then to the right, but the stupid, little key wouldn't budge. I tried wiggling it up and down, which didn't do much besides make a whole lot of metal jangling noise. I needed to get out of this mailroom or my heart would explode. Little chunks of Luella would be plastered all over the mailboxes. I'd ruin so many people's J. Crew catalogues.

And that's what Phil walked into. Hot Phil. Phil, who as it turned out, smelled like sunshine even indoors.

"Hey, you okay?" he asked.

"Fine! I'm fine!" I said, shaking the little key like my life depended on it.

He shook his head and laughed. "These things take a little getting used to. Here, watch. May I?"

I nodded and Phil stepped in, brushing my elbow with the back of his hand. He pushed the key in, lifted it up, and removed it like it was the easiest thing in the world. I felt both embarrassed and angry, 60/40. Also, unfortunately, a little turned on from the hand-to-elbow contact. So more like 60/40/10. The math works because… well, because Luella gives 110%.

"Don't feel bad. It took me, like, three weeks to learn how to do that, and now I'm a show-off," he said.

I tried to laugh but no noise came out. That envelope weighed in my bag like an anvil.

"Hey, what are you doing right now?" he asked, lightly punching my arm.

"Nothing," I said, trying desperately to sound upbeat.

"Let's get a cup of coffee. On me! You can get one of those caramel *mochalooties* with the whipped cream and the pumpkin milk or whatever."

"Mochalooties?" I asked.

"Yeah, they can do mochalooties with soy milk, or almond milk, or pumpkin milk…"

"No way…" I was smiling in spite of myself.

"C'mon, you look like you could use a pumpkin milk with extra pumpkin."

He put his arm around me playfully. I couldn't tell if he was actually charming, or just reminiscent of those cool boys in high school I never stood a chance with. I was exhausted and overwhelmed, and I had just been threatened through the mail, and yet. And yet I felt a flicker of excitement at being taken out to coffee by Hot Phil. And maybe this wasn't a date, maybe Phil knew something about the David G situation. Maybe this was all part of the investigation! It was unlikely, seeing as he was dimmer than a busted lightbulb, but I'd been surprised before.

9

Phil took me to a nearby Starbucks on the *Sex Island* compound. Over pumpkin-flavored lattes, Phil told me goofy stories of his childhood. Finding a lost dog and naming her Stinky, a competitive local turkey trot, climbing to the top of a tall tree only to realize he didn't know how to get down, Wisconsin lore. Talking with Phil felt like a respite. He had such a nice smile. At one point he did hold up a sugar packet and ask me, "What is sugar?" But besides that, he made for fairly good company.

My coffee cup had been empty for a bit. I could have kept sitting there for another couple hours, if I didn't have a murder case to solve and all. He asked if I wanted to get some food.

"I should head back," I told him.

"Damn," he said, revealing that dimple again. He was, unfortunately, unbelievably attractive.

We laughed the whole walk back to the apartment. About what, I have no idea. I looked at the time and realized I'd been off the clock for too long. Crap. We got in the elevator and he pushed the button for the seventh floor.

"You live on seven?" I asked.

"No. You do." He smiled.

"I don't," I said, smiling back at him.

"Yes, you do," he said with a laugh.

"I don't."

"Yes, you do." He was twirling a lock of my wig now. I hoped he didn't realize it was fake.

"I really don't."

He dropped the smile, looking concerned. "Where do you live?"

"Not telling you." I poked his chest. His rock hard chest. And then I saw something like anger flash across his eyes.

The elevator dinged at seven, the doors opened, and neither of us got out.

"Where do *you* live?" I asked him, trying to sound playful. What happened to our mood five minutes ago, I wondered. It suddenly felt tense, like he was going to either kiss or kill me.

Then he held the back of my head and brought me close and kissed me. He tasted like vanilla and smoke. His lips were soft and forceful at the same time. I felt tingly everywhere, like I was melting, like my head was about to float off. It was a fantastic kiss. And then I felt the wig slip under his grasp. Oh, that stupid, stupid wig.

I awkwardly extricated myself, shifting my wig back to the front from where it slipped. He smiled at me. He had my red lipstick smeared all over his mouth.

"I gotta go," I said.

"Okay, I'll take the stairs, you take the elevator. That way we both can keep our secrets for now." He winked at me and backed out, maintaining eye contact as the elevator doors closed on him. "See you on set."

I felt like I was high. I needed to get it together. I was here to solve a murder case. I'd gotten a threatening letter in a mailbox that meant somebody knew where I was, and more disturbingly, who I was. Just then my phone buzzed. To my great relief, it was another text from Sophie:

> *You hear Sex Island David G body found? What ur friend know?*

Nothing, Sophie. Well, nothing *yet.*

10

I got back to my apartment and decided the rest of the day would be a wash. I wasn't thinking straight and figured some sleep might help. I'd start fresh the next day. So, I took out my teeth, hung up my wig, and went to bed at 8 p.m. I woke up the next morning at 5 a.m., my brain abuzz.

FRIDAY

I made a pot of coffee and began to theorize. The apartment smelled vaguely like a woman's perfume, but I didn't think much of it at the time. After a good night's sleep, I already felt better, clearer-headed, ready to solve this thing. I took out a notebook and jotted down what I knew so far. The way I saw it, David G was not a random killing. The fact that he was found dead in my bathroom raised a red flag — this was internal. The only way to get into the building was with a key fob, so that narrowed down the suspects to people who lived in the building. Or friends of people who lived in the building. Or friends of friends of people... Okay, and we were back to square one.

Something about this situation made me think his killer knew him, maybe even knew him well. I remembered there were no visible signs of struggle, except for that strange incision around his bellybutton. I started paging through all the documents the producers gave me. Crew lists, cast lists. There had to be a list of everyone who lived in the building, but the closest I found was a chart of everybody's dietary restrictions.

I checked to see if David G had any allergies... just clams. Murder by clams did seem innovative... but no, no. There would be signs of an allergic reaction. According to the crew list, there were approximately seventy-five people working on the production of *Sex Island*. Then there were the thirty original cast members, which by now had dwindled down to the final seven — eight if you counted me, which I didn't. Perhaps one of the twenty-two disgruntled ex-cast members had returned to seek revenge. But Stephanie and John had claimed there'd been no outside visitors. It seemed like security around here was minimal, but maybe there were measures I wasn't told about.

I thought back to my first day on set — how many crew people had I made regular and direct contact with? The other cast members, the producers, the hair and makeup ladies, and Isa.

Isa was interesting to me. Young, smart, under-appreciated, and overworked. She must've had opportunity, but what motive could she have? Maybe she and David G had something going on the side? Maybe David G was a monster off-camera, and this was her ultimate act of revenge? It was certainly a possibility. I wrote down *Isa* on my list of suspects.

The hair and makeup ladies — Carla and Hannah — were also overworked and under-appreciated, but they didn't strike me as the killing type. They were connected at the hip. If one of them had done it, the other would have known about it. Maybe they did it together? I put both their names under Isa's.

I wondered about the director. I still hadn't met him yet, but I assumed he knew David G pretty well. His name was George Striker, and according to his file, he'd directed every season of *Sex Island* since season three. I knew from the message boards he had a reputation for sleeping with contestants and a "bottomless piña colada policy" while he was on set. Seemed more like a sleazebag than a killer, but I'd hate to underestimate his potential. I wrote his name down and made a note to seek him out once I got to set that day.

I felt strangest about the producers. For some reason Stephanie didn't trust John, and John didn't trust Stephanie. I didn't trust either one of them, and at least one of them didn't trust me. Both were put on the suspect list.

That left me with the cast. So far I'd only really talked with Tasha and Phil. Tasha seemed more sad than anything else, but I'd caught her spying on me twice now, so I couldn't quite rule her out. Frankly, Phil was an attractive idiot, and I wasn't sure how much he was actually capable of besides stacking blocks. Even Legos seemed a bit advanced for Phil.

I'd have to get to know the rest of them: the other women, Sarah and Blair, and the other men, David N, Nate, and Ethan. Being a devoted viewer, I knew Sarah had also slept with David G before coupling with David N. And Nate was best friends with David G for a while, but then David G gave Blair a rim job the same night Nate planned to give Blair a rim job. That drama spanned over three whole episodes. And I remember Ethan tried to form an alliance with Tasha, but just last week, Tasha abandoned him to get back together with David G. It was a tangled web they wove. I threw all their names on the suspect list for good measure.

Suspects:

Isa

Carla and Hannah

George Striker

Stephanie

John

Tasha

Phil

Sarah

Blair

David N

Nate

Ethan

I counted the people on the list — thirteen suspects so far. Any of these people could be a killer, sure, but why? What could David G have done to deserve such a fate? I was knee-deep in thought when I heard a single knock at the door and nearly jumped three feet in the air. I panicked, put a wig on backwards, and ran to look through the peephole. Nobody was there. I slowly opened the door a crack, looked around for any sign of human life, and then I saw it.

A basket of three dozen yellow roses had been left in front of my door. My initial thought was that it was probably a bomb, so I kicked it a few times. Just so we're clear, this was not good bomb protocol. It was very early in the morning, and my judgment was still asleep. After all the kicking, I assumed they were safe and snatched up the card. I opened it so fast, I gave myself a paper cut. The envelope didn't have a name on it, but the note inside was typed. It said:

Can't wait to see you again.

I figured it could've been from the producers, but three dozen roses seemed a little romantic, if so. Strange. Who else knew where I lived? A small, stupid part of me hoped they were from Phil.

11

After getting the flowers, I fell back asleep on the couch. A social worker might say oversleeping when one has so much to do is a poor coping mechanism, but who's got time for that mumbo jumbo when I had so much to do!

I woke up to loud knocking on the door and Isa's bird-like voice chirping.

"Good morning, Luella! We're leaving in five minutes!"

I sat up and rubbed my eyes. The clock said it was already 6 a.m. There is nothing more disorienting than waking up after napping for thirty minutes. D.A.R.E. officers love telling kids about the dangers of drugs, but I think they should also warn them about short morning naps.

We were back on set today, so I took what I call a *gentleman's shower* (don't ask), then stumbled around trying to drink what was left of the coffee and attach my wig at the same time. Not recommended. I think I might've swallowed a bobby pin. Isa knocked again. What the hell happened to those five minutes? I quickly dabbed on some makeup and the result was, unfortunately, Picasso-esque.

"Luella, time to go!"

Maybe Isa was a sadist. I was moving Isa up on the suspect list after this.

I had my hand on the door knob when I realized I'd forgotten my Luella teeth. Definitely needed the teeth. Where on God's green earth were the teeth? Ah yes, they were to the left of the sink. I scampered to the bathroom, but the teeth were not to the left of the sink. Nor were they to the right of the sink or below the sink or even in the toilet. I would gladly contract a case of Giardia at that moment if it meant finding the damned Luella teeth.

Isa knocked again. "Coming!" I screamed using the nicest Disney princess voice I could muster.

I retraced my steps of moving into the new place. I could've sworn I packed the teeth. No matter where I was, I always put the teeth to the left of the sink. Maybe I didn't pack the teeth — maybe they still were upstairs in 7E. But no, I wore them yesterday with Stephanie, with Phil. Where could they possibly be? More Isa knocking. Shit, shit, shit.

"Luella, I'm sorry, we have to go now."

Ugh! And of course today was the day I was supposed to talk with George Striker and all those cast members. The one day I wouldn't be able to open my mouth!

I opened the door, and Isa greeted me with a smile that seemed to say *you're trying my patience*. That morning she wore a long French braid, with not a single hair out of place. This woman got up early and wanted everyone to know it.

"Sorry!" I mumbled, my hand hovering over my mouth. Isa looked down at her clipboard.

"Oh, David G is dead. Producers say it's a suicide. R.I.P. David G."

Isa nodded with her eyes closed, almost like she was mimicking empathy. Suicide was certainly an interesting interpretation of the events.

Isa continued, "So today they're having you guys do an orgy vigil."

"Hmm? A what?" I tried saying without opening my mouth, like an amateur ventriloquist.

"Everyone will say a few words about David G's passing, and then the grief will be too much and the plan is for you all to have an orgy."

Oh no.

"Might be a long day," she added.

That was one way to put it.

12

An orgy vigil. Was I in hell? Isa brought me to my trailer and to no one's surprise, an ungodly costume hung on the back of the chair. Black lace underwear and a veil. Where was the top? Where were the pants? I cleared my throat, pointed at it, and shook my head, which I felt was the universal language for *where is the top? And where are the pants?*

Isa looked at me totally unfazed. "You want a top? Costume department said tops were on request."

I gave her a vigorous head nod.

She held the walkie-talkie to her mouth. "Isa to Wardrobe: Luella wants a top."

Couldn't have said it better myself. She kept the walkie-talkie out, addressing me again. "Any breakfast? Egg whites?"

I shook my head "no" so hard, it was like I was trying to get something off my nose. Then Isa did the strangest thing — she laughed, hard.

"You're a strange one, Luella. I'll be back in ten to take you to set."

She shook her head and trotted off. Okay, so Isa was callous and overworked, but maybe I could find an ally in her yet.

A few minutes later, someone knocked on my trailer door. I had high hopes it was the wardrobe department with a turtleneck. Instead,

I found John wearing a blue chambray shirt that matched his eyes. I noticed it was mis-buttoned. He asked to come in. I nodded. He sat down on the plastic couch, wringing his hands.

"They did the toxicology report. Apparently he'd had a lethal dose of ethylene glycol," he said.

Ethylene glycol, or as it's more familiarly known, antifreeze. You know, the blue stuff you generally pour in your car and not down a human being's gullet.

"Report suggested he'd been dead for up to four days when you found him. Stephanie thought it best to officially call it a suicide for now. She thought telling people he was murdered might make everyone super paranoid, but I don't know. I feel like if you're gonna kill yourself, you don't drink car fluid. Do you think we're doing the right thing here?"

I shrugged.

"You don't think it was a suicide, do you?" he asked.

I shook my head no. He glanced over at my costume still hanging limply on the back of the chair.

"Jeez. If you want, they can get you a shirt."

I gave him the double thumbs up. He cleared his throat and then stood up.

"Well, I'll leave you to it. Wanted you to know the latest." He paused. "Oh! I forgot, I brought you a coffee."

He set down the large paper cup on my dressing table. Funny when someone mentions poison and hands you a drink a moment later.

I needed to know why he didn't want the police involved that night. Why he went along with this whole suicide ruse. Why he looked disheveled on a Friday morning. But finding all that out without speaking was going to nearly impossible. John paused at the doorway and turned to me.

"I'd talk to Nate if you haven't already. Nate and David G were pretty close until the end. Oh, and sorry about the orgy vigil," he shrugged, laughing a little. "Director's idea. Enjoy the coffee!"

John excused himself, gently closing the trailer door behind him. I immediately poured the coffee down the toilet, then panicked as I'd forgotten how to flush it. It was a lever you were supposed to push both up and down with your foot. One way let water in and the other opened a little hole in the bottom of the toilet to move the waste out, and whoever designed this thing had absolutely no regard for human intuition.

A minute later, wardrobe was waiting outside the trailer with what I'd loosely call "a shirt," and I got dressed quickly. It would have to do. All I was thinking about now was Nate. What did John mean when he said, "until the end?" Was he alluding to the Blair rim job debacle of episodes 12-15?

Isa escorted me to set, which was a loft space they'd turned into a porny-looking bedroom. It had a California King-sized bed with black satin sheets and a mirrored ceiling. Nate and Ethan were already there, silently sitting on the bed. I joined them on the opposite side and glanced over at Nate. He was about 6'2" with a baby face, a six-pack, and a buzz cut. The rest of his body he kept fastidiously hairless. He wore a gold chain with a cross on it. Fun fact: Nate was the only practicing Christian on *Sex Island*.

Sitting next to Nate, Ethan looked almost his opposite. He was 5'9" and covered with dark, curly body hair. If the women's testimonials were to be trusted, he had a whopping ten-inch penis. There were rumors online that he wore special ten-inch penis underwear that was custom-made by H&M. Sounded like a difficult life.

A little later, Sarah, Phil, and David N were brought in. Phil winked at me, and I felt my face flush. I looked around and noticed the cameramen had already begun shooting. I was beginning to understand that this show afforded its cast little privacy.

Sarah, the tall blonde whose whole personality was being nice, who once confessed to wearing a 24-karat-gold toe ring she got from "some random guy in Egypt," was the first to speak.

"Did you guys hear they found David G?" she asked, holding a plastic container of what I recognized as the egg whites.

Ethan kept looking at the floor. "Man! It's so sad!"

"I just can't believe it was a suicide," David N said slowly, to no one in particular. He was the skinniest guy on the show and had been trying to grow a goatee for the last month. Online, the fans were pleading for him to shave it off.

Phil sat next to me. "I don't know, guys… you never know what's going on inside someone else's mind."

He started rubbing my shoulders, and I shied away. I liked Phil but I didn't think we'd gotten to the public-shoulder-rubbing stage of our relationship.

"Too hard, babe?" he asked me, with what seemed like genuine concern.

I nodded and stood up, making my way over to a big cooler full of bottled waters. For those wondering, I was still, very unfortunately, without my Luella teeth.

Sarah picked at her egg whites, then threw the whole container in the garbage can (where they belonged).

"Tasha flat-out told the producers she wouldn't be on camera today. Honestly, good for her!" she said.

Ethan chimed in. "Well, she's the one who broke his heart — maybe she feels responsible! Who knows, maybe she *is* responsible!"

Sarah looked at him in shock. "Ethan, that's so not fair!"

Suddenly Blair stormed in, wearing a bright purple feather robe. I noticed it shed, leaving a trail of purple wisps in her wake.

"What the hell, have you guys heard about David G? They found him dead in a random bathroom. Nate, baby, are you okay?"

Nate was full-on crying now. He had a line of snot smeared across his cheek and still somehow managed to look attractive. His shoulders heaved up and down.

"This freakin' sucks!" he bellowed.

I looked up and realized Phil had been watching me this whole time.

"I can't believe Luella just got here. Babe, it's not always like this. Come here, let me hold you," he said, his arms outstretched to me.

I nodded sympathetically, then pretended to find a new mole on my arm. Blair ignored him, continuing on her same train of thought.

"Like, suicide? Is that for real? He is totally not the type."

"There is no type, Blair!" Nate screamed mid-sob.

At that moment, Stephanie walked in with the director, George Striker. Living up to every expectation, George held in his hand a half-empty piña colada. I apologize to the optimists — the piña colada was also, in a way, half-full.

Stephanie cleared her throat. "Hi guys. I just wanted to say that what happened on Wednesday was very tragic. David G was a major part of our community here, and we will all miss him dearly." Then she looked straight at me. "But he decided to end his life and we can't do anything about that."

Why was she lying? And why was she specifically addressing me?

George continued, using a surprisingly fake British accent. "I know it's hard, but this is show business, and the show must crack on, right? So we're going to have a vigil for David G here in the bedroom, and if the grief moves you, you can have community sex afterwards, and then we'll call it for the day." He truly sounded like a cartoon chimney sweep. Did this guy really think that was a convincing accent?

Everyone was silent. Then Blair asked the question I assumed was on everyone's mind: "What's community sex?"

Stephanie was terse in her response. "Like an orgy, Blair. We're trying to be sensitive about David G."

Blair crossed her arms and sat on the bed, sending a flurry of tiny purple feathers everywhere. "Well, I don't feel like having sex."

George exhaled. "That's fine, Blair, you don't have to have sex. Just don't get in the way of everyone else having a good, healing time."

Nate wiped his nose on his hairless arm. "I don't wanna have sex, either. I'm just too sad to get hard."

Sarah added, "Yeah, if anything, I'll cuddle, but I'm not having sex. Sorry, George. Sorry, Steph."

Was I witnessing a coup?

"I'll do it," Phil said, looking right at me. Jeez, *this* guy.

"Thank you, Phil. Love you, buddy," George said, giving Phil a little head pat.

Stephanie spoke through clenched teeth. I could almost see the hot steam shooting out of her ears.

"Thank you, Phil. And the rest of you can cuddle, that's just great! That's exactly what people want to see, and that's what you're paid to do. Why don't you put on sweatpants while you're at it? Share a big bowl of Doritos?! Slather barbecue sauce on your faces and complain about your taxes!" She stormed out of the room, then paused right outside the door. "Luella, can I have a word?"

Uh-oh. I followed her out of the bedroom into the hallway. George Striker stayed with the cast and started camera blocking. Stephanie and I were surrounded by busy crew members preparing for the morning's shoot. I noticed her neck was flushed and her hands were shaking.

"Found something of yours," she said. Stephanie reached into her jacket pocket and pulled out my tooth case. She rattled it for good measure.

That perfume smell this morning. It was orange, amber, and something else. Was that Stephanie's perfume?

I raised my eyebrows. "Where did you —" I began to ask, but she cut me off.

"I don't trust you," she continued.

Well, that makes two of us, I thought. How and when did she get that, I wondered. I inhaled and thought I smelled amber. Then I snatched the tooth case out of her hands before she could think to do anything otherwise.

"You know, we get a lot of crazy fans doing crazy things to be on this show," she said, her voice guttural.

Did she realize that *she was the one who asked me* to do this?

She continued, "I tried to find your paperwork. Payroll said you asked to be paid in cash. That you refused to put a Social Security

MURDER ON SEX ISLAND

number on file. I don't know what you're trying to pull, but whatever it is, I'm gonna find out and I'm gonna put a stop to it."

I held her gaze. Stephanie's teeth were clenched. She gave me a tense nod then walked away. I stood there in disbelief. What had just happened? I looked around and saw Isa standing there. She must've heard everything. I'd have to make her my ally sooner than I thought.

13

I snuck into a closet to pop my Luella teeth back in, then returned to the porny room to find the cast quietly cuddling on the bed. It looked almost cozy if you removed 100% of the context. Occasionally Isa would pull someone off the bed for a filmed confessional. Those took place in another room, so I couldn't hear much, but Nate came back from his red-eyed and sniffling.

Ultimately, the orgy vigil was a bust. The group ended up holding each other for about three hours. Eventually Isa came in and told us the editors were just gonna put moaning sounds over footage of melting candles, and that we could all go home.

An hour later I got a text from a number I didn't know. It simply said:

meet at Cantina, 5pm. Tell no one.

I figured this was the infamous Cantina Stephanie had mentioned. At 5 p.m., the sun would still be out. If someone *was* trying to hurt me, doing it in broad daylight would not be ideal. I decided to go. Someone wanted to meet with Luella. Maybe this was an informant.

I left the apartment building around 4:30 and had a nagging feeling someone was watching me. I knew technically we weren't supposed to leave the compound, but since I wasn't actually part of the cast, I felt above the rules in some respects. Besides, with the Luella teeth safely back in my mouth, I had a little spring in my step even if that interaction with Stephanie left me shaken. Whoever asked me to meet them at Cantina might know something to help solve the case.

I arrived at the bar at exactly 5:01 p.m. From the outside, Cantina looked like any other dive bar. Neon signs for lite beer were suspended in the windows, and the front door looked like it was used to being kicked open. An older man smoked a thin cigar near the front and looked me up and down as I walked in. He gave me the creeps. If this were a video game, I would've split-punched him. You know, one of those things where you do the splits and punch someone in the groin from below? Works like a charm in video games. If only everything were as cut and dry.

I walked further into the bar. The space was dark, much darker than it was outside. The floors were sticky, with a quicksand-like quality. If my shoes stayed put for too long, it became difficult to move forward. My mind spiraled through all the substances that could have made a floor so sticky — spilled margaritas, semen, a lifetime supply of chewed Juicy Fruit. The smell of bleach competed with the smell of stale beer. It was a close call, but it seemed stale beer would take the win that evening.

I looked around for any recognizable face. A husky man with a long gray beard and a beat-up leather jacket played a slow game of darts against himself. The bartender, wearing a tank top and board shorts, was busy cleaning his left ear with his pointer finger. I made a mental note to avoid ordering any drink he'd have to squeeze something into.

I was starting to feel like I'd been pranked or set up, when I felt a tap on my shoulder. I turned to find Sarah, blonde, tall, and smiling at me. She gave me a big hug.

"I'm so glad you got my text! Yay! Come in, we're in the back."

Maybe it wasn't so bad Sarah was nice.

I followed her into a backroom, where David N, Nate, Blair, and Tasha were sitting around an old wooden table sharing a pitcher of beer. No Ethan, no Phil. I was surprised to see Tasha there. Her long black hair was up in a messy bun, and she didn't look like she'd slept much the last couple nights.

Blair looked up at me. "New girl, want some beer?"

I nodded, and she poured me a glass of mostly foam. I sat in the small space between Nate and Sarah and took a sip. Oh goodie, it was just how I liked it: very warm. Everyone seemed to be about two beers in, by which I mean they were coherent but loose. Nate turned toward me, his golden cross gleaming in the low light. His eyes were still red-rimmed and he spoke about an inch from my face.

"Lula, it's so bad here."

Tasha corrected him. "Nate, her name is Luellie, like Julie with a 'lellie.'"

These were real creatives I was dealing with here.

"Why's it bad?" I asked Nate.

"They killed David G. He was too beautiful, so they killed him." He began to weep and put his head on the table. Sarah rubbed his hairless shoulders.

"Who do you think killed him?" I figured it couldn't hurt to ask.

Tasha poured herself another beer. "I bet it was that producer, Stephanie. She wanted him, and she couldn't have him, so she killed him."

David N spoke up then. In the dim bar lighting, his sparse goatee almost looked filled in. "Wait! I thought they were already sleeping together."

"No," Tasha said sharply. "But she definitely wanted him."

"Well, everybody wanted him," Blair added. I saw Nate look to her. She avoided his glance.

"What's with John?" I asked.

Nobody responded. Sarah looked around, then answered for the group. "He's… John's fine."

"Did you guys know he's from the same town as David G? I think they were, like, family friends or something. That's what Stephanie told me," David N added.

I considered this information. When it came to John, it seemed Stephanie was quite the talker.

Nate slammed his beer down. "You know what's so messed up about all this? Two weeks ago, David G told me he got a call from an acting agent."

David N looked up from his beer. "Wait, he did? For real?"

"Shit, that's so sad," Blair said, slamming down her empty beer mug. "But, like, also, is this killer gonna strike again? If they got David G, who's next?"

"I'm sure it's just a one-time thing," David N stammered.

"Maybe it's a plan to kill the top contestants. Who would be next? Like me? Am I next?" Tasha's voice was getting shaky.

"Tasha, calm down! David G lost his life, let's not go nuts here!" Nate yelled.

Tasha shook her head. "But he was gonna win. Everybody knew that. He and I, we were gonna win. So, where does that leave me?"

Sarah reached out and held Tasha's hand. "Shh, Tasha, it's okay. There's no telling if you were gonna win this thing. I'm sure you're safe." Sarah then looked at me. "Lulie, you know how people win this show, right?"

I shook my head no and hoped it was convincing. Sarah's eyes lit up.

"Okay, you are *in* for it. Basically you try to have sex with as many people as possible, and then you're voted on to the next round by how good your sex was. But if you betray someone, that person might say the sex with you was bad, even if the sex with you was actually really good. That happened with Rachel and Michael during Week One. Do you guys remember? Michael was so good at sex but then he slept with Blair which was very rude to Rachel, so then Rachel said he was bad at sex and didn't make her cum, even though he made her cum twice!"

"So sad," Blair repeated into her mug. "Rachel had Crohn's Disease, which was hard for all of us. She was, like, always in the bathroom."

"Right, so in order to win, you have to be good at sex and nice enough so that when you do have sex with other people, the person you had sex with first is, like, chill about it. Do you follow?" Sarah asked.

I nodded.

"You have to be, like, hot and chill. Which is really hard to do because they sleep-deprive us, and sometimes they give us, like, a ton of alcohol and no food for hours on end." Sarah looked at the nearly empty pitcher. "Wait, should we get another one?"

Blair picked up where Sarah left off. "Basically what Sarah's saying is that David G was special. Everyone could see it. And he was really good at sex."

"So good at sex," Tasha and Sarah said almost in unison.

I thought I saw David N make eyes at Nate, but when I looked again they were both nodding sympathetically.

"Wow," I said and took a sip. My beer was actually hot now, but I choked it down. "Where are Ethan and Phil?"

"We never see Phil outside of set," David N answered. "And I don't know where Ethan is. He didn't respond to the group text."

"The group text?" I asked.

They all looked to each other. I felt like I wasn't getting invited to a birthday party in real time.

"If you add somebody to the group text, does that mean they get to see the texts that came before they were added to it?" Sarah asked.

"I don't think so," Nate answered.

Sarah took in this information with a slow nod. "Well, we can add you, if you want," she coolly offered.

"Thanks!" I said. I figured getting on the group text could not *not* help the case. In my estimation, I had one more question before they started accusing me of having *investigation vibes*.

"Why don't you see Phil?" I asked.

"He kinda keeps to himself. Works out a lot. I think he likes you, though," David N said with a smile.

"He definitely likes you. You should sleep with him. He's kinda cute in a grown-up boy band member kinda way," Sarah added.

Sage advice from the masters themselves. I told them I'd think about it.

The night ended with everyone drunkenly staggering from cabs into the apartment complex, shushing each other and giggling. If this was breaking the rules, no one here seemed to give a damn about consequences. I got back to my room, and immediately my phone buzzed. I had been added to the group chat. I recognized Sarah's number as the first text:

LULEEEEEE!!!!

The rest came in quick succession from the other five numbers. I tried deducing who was who using my ace detective skills (I was only a little buzzed on warm beer).

Hi Bitches (Blair, or possibly Tasha)

I'm horny (David N, or maybe Nate)

Does any1 have food? (Nate, or maybe David N)

I have half a bag of Doritos (David N, or possibly Nate)

Ew grow up (Tasha, or possibly Blair)

Where's the caviar bitch (Blair, or possibly Tasha)

Figuring out people's numbers felt like drunkenly solving a Sudoku puzzle. I noticed both Ethan and Phil were left off. Was it because they'd missed the drinks outing? Or did it go deeper than that? The group text continued throughout the night, fueled mostly by people calling other people bitches. I was starting to regret asking to be put on this thing.

SATURDAY

Saturday morning I woke up and realized it was already Saturday afternoon. I lay in bed wondering where my cats were until I remembered I was on an island, a man had been poisoned, and there was a killer on the loose. Before I could begin to wallow in my guilt spiral, I got on my Luella gear and headed out to determine where — if anywhere — a murder could take place around here. Of the Means, Motive, and Opportunity trio, today I would laser in on the big O. By which I meant Opportunity, not orgasm, though I understand how given the circumstances... whatever.

I slowly made my way from the apartment building to the crew parking lot. Where could you kill someone? And where could you hide a dead body for up to four days?

Seeing the huge lot devoid of people was strange. The utter stillness of the trailers, trucks, and equipment gave the place a ghost town feel. I wondered if anybody ever checked the trailers at night or over the weekends for that matter; if they were even locked.

Everyone's trailer had their name printed on a star that was fixed to their door, just like a nursery school would. I ambled through the rows of trailers and found myself in front of Phil's. As I walked up the metal grate stairs, they squeaked loudly. So much for being discreet.

I tried his door, and it turned out to be locked. Then I looked to the flimsy windows. Surely those weren't so secure. I grabbed some *apple boxes* that were lying around — these were basic wooden boxes you could sit or stand on or stack things on top of. I don't know why they called them apple boxes. Maybe in old Hollywood, they served a double purpose of also storing fruit for the hungry cameramen.

I stacked up a few apple boxes until I was at eye level with Phil's window. Then using the heel of my palm, I popped out the plastic window pane. It fell inside the trailer, clattering to the ground while remaining intact. For all the evils of plastic, it really is a boon for the breaking-and-entering community.

With ample grunting and something I could only refer to as "squelching," I was finally able to hoist my body inside. I cursed myself for not having more upper body strength. Luckily I landed with a nice thud on the couch. It smelled like Phil in there. Coconut, vanilla, sunshine. I tried to put the kiss out of my mind.

His trailer was larger than mine, with room for a recliner chair and a bigger fridge. I looked inside — rows upon rows of Gatorades and a Tupperware containing six peeled hard-boiled eggs. His trash had been emptied. I startled myself catching my reflection in the mirror. I realized I didn't know quite what I was looking for, and I was jumpy. If the trash was taken out, that meant people came by to clean it regularly, which meant a dead body couldn't just hang out in there for days. Then my eyes wandered up to a photograph tucked into the top right corner of the vanity.

It was an old, wallet-sized portrait of a woman. From her fashion choices and hairdo, I guessed the photo was taken in the mid-1980s. She looked to be about 18 years old, fresh-faced, pretty. To be honest, she looked a little like Phil — same brown eyes, same long lashes. Maybe she was his mother, or a beloved aunt, or possibly a younger photograph of his much older girlfriend. I wanted to find out more about Phil. He intrigued me. And it wasn't like that, I didn't just want… Alright, I'm the storyteller here. We're moving on.

I left Phil's trailer feeling like I'd just violated his space for nothing. I put the window pane back in and left through the door like a civilized human being. I had to leave it unlocked, but I figured it didn't matter much with the window being removable. I mean, someone could break in even if they had no upper body strength whatsoever! What else could be done around here if someone with wet-noodle arms had a killer's instinct?

I was carrying the apple boxes back to where I'd found them when I heard two men's voices arguing. I quickly hid behind Phil's trailer and listened.

"Don't tell me what to do!" yelled one man.

"Bro, I'm not! I just want to do it right," said the other.

I recognized the first voice as Nate's. The second I couldn't place. The voices got closer and angrier, until they stopped entirely. I looked up to find Nate and Ethan staring at me, as I crouched against the trailer's metal siding.

"What are you doing here?" Ethan asked me gruffly.

"I'm... lost," I said. "The apartment building is...?"

"Over there," Nate said, pointing to the only building taller than two stories within a mile. I nodded and stood, my knees cracking on the way up. Nate quickly looked at Ethan.

"We can take you, if you want," he said.

"I'm good," I said, already heading in the direction of the apartment building. Once I was twenty feet away, I looked back. The two of them were standing there watching me. I quickly walked some more, and when I looked back again, they were gone.

SUNDAY

I spent Sunday poring over the suspects in my notebook. Stephanie was rising on my list. So was John. But why would a producer of a hit show kill their star? David G was a well-known catch — and a front-runner to win *Sex Island*. What would either of them stand to gain by killing him? Nate and Ethan were acting very strange near the trailers, and I couldn't quite rule out Tasha yet. Who among them had access to antifreeze? And most importantly, who had access to David G?

Then suddenly, I thought again of Isa. How was it she seemed to be everywhere at once? And what did she know? I searched through the box the producers had given me and found her file.

Isa was 22 years old and originally from Michigan. Her resumé before *Sex Island* was spotty— she'd been a manager at a frozen yogurt shop and a barista in college. She went to NYU for film. I couldn't imagine that being a production assistant on *Sex Island* was her dream job. I tried looking her up online. No social media accounts, almost no online presence except for a senior thesis film that was available on Vimeo. The film showed a young woman crying as a naked older man did some type of modern dance behind her. There was no dialogue, only soft ambient music. From what I could gather, the plot was loosely, *a couple breaks up.*

I realized while watching her film that these last couple days were the longest I'd gone without actually watching *Sex Island*. I wondered if there were any clues in the episodes leading up to David G's disappearance — maybe something that I hadn't given significance to before.

Like I'd done countless times before, I began a *Sex Island* marathon. I decided to start with the Friday before I arrived. The last person to admit to seeing David G was Tasha, and that was Saturday night. He was found dead Wednesday evening and the coroner said he'd been dead for up to 96 hours. So chances were that David G was killed sometime between late Saturday night and early Sunday morning.

That Friday episode was surreal to watch, mostly because David G was still alive in it. He wore a gray T-shirt and scrubs, which seemed a little overkill now that I knew there was a costume department. Why not just stick a sign on his back that said *MALE NURSE*?

He stood near the Hibiscus Arch whispering to Tasha, who was giggling and swatting at him. In this shot, they really looked like lovebirds, not at all like a couple that would get into a big fight that day. Certainly not a broken-up couple. I guess who really knew anything, though. I'm sure my ex-husband and I looked happy at least some of the time.

Blair and Sarah were lying out in adjacent beach chairs, while Nate and David N took turns seeing who could jump up and touch higher on a small palm tree. Phil was off to the side doing push-ups. I started to wonder where Ethan was when the camera cut to him, lurking behind a cabana and glowering in the direction of David G and Tasha.

They cut to Ethan's confessional. He wore an unzipped hoodie with nothing underneath and spoke directly to camera.

"I'm not mad. Tasha and David G can do whatever they want. Listen, when you've got ten inches, there's plenty to go around." His eyes shifted to the person standing beside the camera, and he gave whoever it was an antagonistic smile.

The camera cut to a confessional with David G. I noticed in this close-up, under the bright lights, his skin looked gray and I could see bags under his eyes through the layers of makeup. He spoke directly to camera.

"I'm having a great time. Tasha and I are back on track. I know Ethan's upset, but Tasha's a grown woman and she can do whoever she wants. And she picked me, suckers!"

With that, David G ripped off his gray T-shirt and waved it around his head, laughing. I paused the episode, dragging the mouse back and forth to examine the footage a few seconds before and after this moment. Very interesting, indeed. Whoever cut around David G's navel did it after this episode was taped.

14

MONDAY

Monday morning, our call time was pushed up to 5:30 a.m. When the cast arrived on set, we were told that push "was a mistake" — that the crew would be arriving at 6 a.m., as usual. Perhaps the cast was being collectively punished for refusing to do the orgy vigil. Isa stormed off to make some passive-aggressive phone calls.

That early in the morning, just before sunrise, the sky, water, and sand all shared the same color palette. Some variation on slate blue. It was almost chilly, and there was a new layer of dew on the sides of the trailers. The entire cast was grumbling and cursing. It was only a half-hour earlier than usual, but time felt like gold when one had a full shoot day ahead of them. I saw David N kick a tire then limp away. I noticed Tasha was back on set, seeming a little worse for the wear. She slumped down to the ground and pulled her sun hat low on her head.

Ethan was the first to speak up. "Guys, it's only a half hour. Let's just hang here. By the time we get back to our apartments, it'll be time to leave again."

Everyone grumbled in agreement. In the morning haze, Ethan had become our de facto leader. I wondered if he enjoyed his modicum of power, and if he had ever been tempted to abuse it.

Blair tried to get in her trailer. Finding it locked, she let out a beleaguered groan. Phil tried his and found it open. I held my breath.

"Hey, how come yours is open and mine isn't?" Blair asked him.

I saw Nate and Ethan look to each other, then look right at me.

"I don't know. Sucks for everyone else!" Phil said as he trotted inside and slammed the door behind him. I was so grateful he was stupid.

The other trailers were locked, so everyone besides Phil milled around within a ten-foot radius. I took this opportunity to approach the ten-inch king. Ethan was sitting on his trailer stairs cleaning his nails as I approached.

"How was the rest of your Sunday?" I asked him.

He gave me the up-and-down then went back to his fingernails. "What's up?"

"Being new... it's a lot to learn," I said.

"You shouldn't be on set over the weekends," he said, now cleaning his thumb.

"Why were you here?" I asked.

Ethan exhaled. "Look, I get that you're coming in pretty late in the season, and you're not exactly the show's type, no offense, but I'd mind my own business if I were you."

"Anything else?" I asked.

"Just avoid alliances." Still, he wouldn't look up.

"Why?" I asked.

"Alliances end badly on this show."

MURDER ON SEX ISLAND

He finally looked me in the eyes. Maybe it was the morning chill, but my upper arms broke out in goosebumps. I wondered if Ethan had wanted David G dead.

"What happened with Tasha?" I asked.

"I said mind your own business, didn't I? Now put a sweater on, your arms look weird." With that, he got up and walked toward the beach. What a ten-inch dick.

Phil must've left his trailer, because when I turned, he was standing right in front of me. I was startled.

"Did I surprise you?" he asked, smiling.

"Sure did."

He was lightly kicking sand that had made its way onto the parking lot.

"So you like Ethan?"

"He's fine," I said.

Phil cleared his throat. "Um… Luella… Man, this feels crazy to ask you." He shadow-boxed for a moment, then turned to me looking very serious. "Would you wanna form an alliance with me?"

"What?"

He took my hand. "I just love your look, and you're so hot… and I think you're really attractive."

Okay, it turned out Phil was a poet. I realized my mouth was hanging open in shock so I closed it and forced a smile.

"No, do it with teeth," he said.

He put his finger between my lips and pushed my top lip up and my bottom lip down. I started laughing, but not because it was funny. I knew he was the weird one in this situation, but I couldn't help feeling anxious that my teeth would feel false and my lips would feel rough. Crushes really do turn people's brains to mush. If possible, they should be avoided at all costs. Not that I had a crush on Phil. I didn't. Because that would be absolutely unprofessional and bad.

"Today they're asking us to pair up and have sex and declare our sexual allegiance to another contestant," Phil said to me, maintaining direct eye contact, his fingers still on my lips. He was so gorgeous, I swear I actually felt weak in the knees. His eyes were the color of good coffee. His breath smelled like mouthwash. He wore a baseball shirt, cut-off jean shorts, and those awful Prada flip-flops. I noticed his toes were pedicured this time. Every part of his body was toned and muscular. Damn. Damn, damn, damn.

I want to say this. I came to this island to find a missing man, and that's what I intended to do. And from an outsider's perspective I could see how one would start to wonder stuff like... *Does she ever work? Is she about to have sex with a 20-year-old? What kind of investigation is this? And how is she swimsuit-ready if she came from a winter in New York City?*

All terrific questions, really. The answers are: yes, maybe, I don't know anymore, and anyone can be "swimsuit-ready" if they put on a swimsuit and maintain a constant out-of-body headspace.

I stared at this young Adonis and considered my options. The question of the sexual alliance hung between us like subway smell. The sandwiches or the train. Either one has the terrific power to linger.

A basic audit of my logic at that moment:

Should I have sex with this man? I don't know.

Was I several years older than him, not to the point where I could be his mother but to the point where I could be his young aunt? Yes.

Did he think of me like that woman in the photograph on his mirror? Maybe.

Would sleeping with him give me more information? Maybe. Probably. Definitely. Probably. Maybe. No. Absolutely not.

Maybe.

Had I slept with someone since my ex-husband? No.

Did I have horrible, actually awful, gut-wrenching taste in men? Yes.

"I'll do it," I said to him. Phil smiled and his dimple appeared again. At that point, the dimple felt practically Pavlovian to me. He gave me another one of those sex hugs and whispered in my ear, "See you on set." Then he walked off toward the beach, essentially taking my genitals with him.

I stood there, realizing what I'd just said yes to. That's when Isa marched through, proudly announcing she had acquired the keys to the trailers. As she let me in mine, I heard her muttering, "Where would any of you be without me."

Once I was inside my trailer, I looked in the mirror. I had sweat through my clothes and my wig was askew. With my finger, I lifted my lips like Phil had done. I felt my Luella teeth, wondering if he'd also noticed how fake they were.

15

By 8 a.m., the crew was ready to shoot. Isa escorted the cast to the beach hut. We were placed in a circle and given tropical drinks. Mine tasted like watered-down rum and had a sad maraschino cherry floating in it. Phil stood to my right. His left hand grabbed my right hand and held it there. My palm started sweating, but his stayed cool and dry. From across the circle, Sarah wiggled her eyebrows at me.

Minutes later, George Striker strutted in. He wore a button-down shirt completely unbuttoned and a newly minted Manchester United cap.

"Hello, my children! Sorry about the mix-up this morning. As usual, blame Isa!" he announced in his fake British accent.

I glanced over at Isa, who was smiling with her mouth but not her eyes. I realized Isa probably shoveled a lot of shit around here.

Striker made a beeline to me and introduced himself. I've included his pronunciation just to give you a sense of how truly awful his accent was.

"I'm George (Johj), the director (directah). I see you may be pairing (peh-ring) up with young Phil here (hea). Good work (wuck)." The queen was rolling in her grave.

Somehow, he had more to say. "I always like to get to know the new cast members. Luella, meet me for a pint at my flat after work. 5 p.m."

I looked to Sarah, and she nodded. Perhaps this was standard procedure.

"Sure, 5 p.m.," I told him. Striker left me with a slimy feeling all over.

He spun around and addressed the group. "We're partnering up today, so make good choices, children! And action!"

Moments later, the cameras were rolling. Phil chose me, Sarah chose David N, and Nate chose Blair. Ethan chose Tasha, which I thought was interesting considering their failed alliance. Maybe it hadn't failed after all.

Each couple was taken to a separate cabana room, along with two cameramen and a sound guy. Phil put his hand on my lower back and whispered, "This is going to be fun!" It occurred to me then that every decision I'd made leading up to this one had been wrong. I wasn't supposed to be here. Not at all.

The cabana room turned out to be basically a yurt. Everything was cream-colored. I'd call it asylum-chic. The walls — already a generous term — were made of sturdy linen and were tented at the top to form a roof, another generous term. Inside there was a bed, two small potted palm trees, and a pole. As the pole was not connected to anything else, I presumed it was there for dancing purposes.

One of the cameramen positioned us in the bed. Phil and I were both put on our sides, facing the same direction. Then Phil was pushed closer to me, and I was officially the little spoon. The cameraman draped Phil's arm over my shoulder, checked something in his view finder, then came back and brushed some hair out of my face.

He went back to his camera and shouted, "Whenever you're ready!"

"Camera rolling," the other cameraman said.

"Sound rolling," the sound guy yelled.

I froze. My brain was blank, and my body was numb. I could feel my eyelid start to spasm — always a sign of confidence. I prayed for a natural disaster. If this was being a private detective, I would return to social work tomorrow. I had no plan for this. Why didn't I think of this having-sex-on-TV part? I could feel the three-man crew growing impatient. Did Phil expect me to make the first move? My breathing got faster. There I was, with four men in a yurt who were all waiting for me to have sex with one of them. I'd said it before and I was sure I'd say it again, but this particular moment had to be my worst nightmare.

Before I knew what was happening, Phil pulled the bed's duvet cover over us, got on top of me and moaned. Then a couple seconds later, he moaned again. He gyrated, he quivered, he grunted, and he called out my name. I double checked — my clothes were still on and so were his. He actually hadn't even touched me.

"Are you close?" he gasped.

I was utterly confused. Then he winked at me. So, it was all fake? A wave of relief came over me.

"Yes?" I said, winking back at him.

He moaned louder now and asked again. "Are you close?!"

"Uh-huh!" I grunted, rolling my eyes back for good measure.

He screamed out, "Luella! Youuuuur pusssssssy!"

"Thank youuuuuu!" I yelled.

His air humps were enormous. He gave me the look again.

"Your dick. Your dick is... your dick!" Yep. That is, unfortunately, what I said. You can check the tapes.

"My dick is inside you!" Phil added. A real yes-and moment! This guy was a true professional. "It feels so gooooood!"

Then he tapped my shoulder two times, and by some miracle, I understood implicitly what this signal meant.

"Ah, ah, ah," I said.

"Oh, oh!" he yelled.

"That's it. I'm coming now," I said, hoping it wasn't as unconvincing as it sounded in my head.

"I'm coming!" he screamed. "I'm coming buckets!"

And then he gasped and fell beside me on the bed. He rolled over and kissed me on the cheek. In all my life, it was the single best cheek kiss I'd ever received.

"Sleep," he whispered. And so we faked that, too. He spooned me, and there we pretended to sleep for over an hour until our little three-man crew got bored and decided to get B-roll of ocean waves, and if they were lucky, little crabs scuttling over a log.

When they were gone, I turned around to face Phil.

"What was that?" I asked.

"TV sex," he said.

"It's not real?" I asked.

"I can't speak for anyone else, but not with me," he said.

"Huh," I smiled. I felt a strange intimacy with him now.

He got out of bed. "C'mon, let's go get some cold cuts. I need my protein fix."

I followed him out, then looked back at what our fake sex had done to the bed. Pretty convincing, I'd say.

16

After his "protein fix," Phil and I parted ways. He went to work out, and I decided to pay a visit to my second-least favorite *Sex Island* producer. I'd heard John took lunch alone in his office, so I figured I'd meet him there. The producers' offices were in the building I'd visited that first night on the island, the one with all the beige carpeting. It wasn't far from the set but the walk was entirely uphill, which I couldn't help but feel was metaphoric.

John was in his office when I arrived, eating an unruly tuna salad sandwich. In a battle of tuna vs. bread, the tuna was winning by a long shot. This was the kind of sandwich you ate alone, and if anyone happened to see you eat it, you'd have to kill them. Perhaps David G saw John eating an equally enormous tuna salad sandwich, and that is why John... I'm sorry, it's never appropriate to joke about the dead. Rest in peace, John's self-respect.

John was so shocked to see me, he quickly wiped his mouth with his sleeve and shoved the remainder of his sandwich in a desk drawer.

"What's up?" he coughed, then cleared his throat three times in a row. Something was in there, and if I had to guess, it was tuna. Luella van Horn, professional detective.

I sat down in one of the two chairs across from him. "You knew David G from before?"

"Who said that?" John wiped his mouth again.

"A few people," I said. "Why didn't you say something?"

"Well, we're technically family friends. I didn't think it was worth mentioning."

"Any bad blood?" I asked.

"No, nothing like that. He was pretty much a baby when I was already in middle school. I didn't know David G so well, mostly just his older sister, Francis, and their parents."

John started folding a paper napkin into smaller and smaller squares.

"You still talk to them?"

John nodded. "Yeah, I reached out once the body was found. I should've told them earlier, but I didn't want to worry anybody when he first went missing. I admit, I messed that up." He coughed again. "So, what brings you in?"

"What's with Ethan?"

John seemed visibly relieved for the change of subject. "He's pretty self-sufficient, has good ratings. Last I checked he was in the top three."

"Top three?" I asked.

"Yeah, every week we have viewers vote on who they like," John clicked around on his computer. "Ethan's been in the top three for the last two weeks. Right now, it looks like Ethan's in third, then Phil and then Tasha."

John turned the screen toward me. It was a line graph with every cast member on the X-axis and audience approval on the Y-axis. I knew about the voting from my time on the message boards, but I hadn't realized the extent to which the producers were tracking the data. I vainly scanned the graph for my name and found I'd rated just above Sarah and below Nate. Okay, not bad! David N was at the very bottom, which didn't surprise me much. He really needed to shave that goatee.

John saw where I was looking. "For a detective doing an undercover thing, you're actually doing pretty well."

My heart stopped. So, it was John who knew about Marie. "What'd you say?"

"You're a detective and you're pretending to be a contestant... did I say something wrong?"

"Right, right," I said, trying to laughing it off. If John didn't send the card, maybe he sent the bouquet. "Hey, thanks for the flowers."

"You know, usually when a woman thanks me for flowers, I just pretend to know something about it. But in the spirit of transparency, whatever flowers you got weren't from me. Based on today's footage, maybe they were from ol' Phil!"

I considered this possibility and tried not to smile.

"He fakes the sex," I added, hoping this wasn't new information to him.

"Yeah. I think it's pretty smart. You wouldn't believe what goes on around here. One week everybody, and I mean everybody, got Syphilis." John shook his head.

"He's the only one...?" I asked.

"Yep. The women seem to appreciate it, though. Everyone else does it for real, I'm pretty sure. The things I have seen sitting in that edit bay..." he chuckled, then stopped himself. "Oh you wanna see something nuts?" He clicked around on his computer again, opening a folder marked CONFIDENTIAL.

On the screen was a photo of a young boy in red swim trunks standing on a beach. He looked to be about six or seven years old. He was chubby and rosy-cheeked, with long eyelashes, only two visible teeth, and a prominent outie bellybutton. He looked vaguely familiar.

"Who's that?" I asked.

"Guess!" John said. He was excited now.

"I don't know," I said.

John put his elbows on his desk and leaned toward me. "Would you believe that was Phil?"

I was shook. I looked again. Were those the same brown eyes I'd just seen an hour ago? It was possible.

John chuckled again. "As Phil started taking off in the ratings, someone from his past put this online and as you can imagine, it circulated pretty quick. Anyway, he got upset and demanded we "control the narrative." His words. So, that's when Ethan's ten-inch penis rumor came out."

"Not true?" I asked, albeit a little too genuinely.

"No, it's actually eleven inches. Har har." John smiled at me.

"Dirty business," I said.

"Dirty show," he retorted.

"How were the ratings after David G disappeared?" I asked.

John nervously laughed. "Uh... they've been... well, the network has been very pleased."

What a business model. I stood to go. John stood, too.

"Luella, before you go, I thought maybe this could be of some help."

He pulled a piece of paper from a file folder and handed it to me. It was a handwritten list of names and apartment numbers:

~~David G - 7A~~

Ethan - ~~7E~~ 8A

David N - 7B

Phil - 7G

Nate - 7C

Blair - 7D

Tasha - 7H

Sarah - 4D

George - PH

Stephanie - 7F

John - 2A

Isa- 8D

Luella - ~~7E~~ 4E

"Stephanie said giving this to you would be an invasion of privacy, but I figure it couldn't hurt your investigation to know where everybody lives."

I looked it over and thanked him.

"Hey, uh, what you saw in here today, that's between us," John added.

"The tuna?" I asked.

He turned pink and laughed. "Yeah, the Phil photo, the ratings, and also the tuna…"

I nodded to his desk. "Careful. Your drawer's getting ripe."

Were we flirting? I told myself to stop flirting with tuna man, and to stop it right now. This show was pickling my brain.

I left John's office feeling a certain sympathy for Phil. Here he was years later trying to be some hot guy on TV, but someone from his past wouldn't let him escape. In some ways, I could relate. I felt my phone buzz, and a small part of me hoped it was Phil wanting to hang out or talk or have a practice round of air sex. I checked and no such luck. Just two texts from Sophie:

> *New guys coming on SI tomorrow. Hot guys!!!! Tell ur frien*
>
> *Ur stinky cats still alive*

New cast members were being added. Strange, John hadn't mentioned that.

17

After meeting with John, I sat on the beach for a while to organize my thoughts. So, new men were coming on the show. Why not new women? Was this the producers' messed up way of getting the viewers to move on from the David G tragedy? After learning what they'd done with Ethan's penis, I assumed they were capable of anything. My stomach started rumbling, and I looked at the time. It was already 4 p.m. I had about an hour to eat and change my clothes before paying a visit to the jolly old chap, George Striker, at 5 p.m.

I ambled back to the apartment complex, smelling the salt in the air. The temperature on the island tended to cool down after 3 p.m. At that moment, it was a perfect 70 degrees with a gentle breeze and a still-warm sun low in the sky. Despite, you know, a murderer on the loose and the dead 21-year-old found in my bathtub and hell, let's throw in the stifling humidity, it was very pleasant there.

I was about a hundred feet away from the apartment building when I started to hear footsteps behind me. I paused, and the footsteps also paused. I turned around, but there was no one there. I walked faster toward the entrance — as fast as I could in 4.5-inch wedge heels. From the sound of my follower's steps, they were wearing a sandal of some kind. Maybe a flip-flop. By the time I got to the entranceway, my heart was pounding.

I stood there for a moment, bracing myself on the stucco exterior of the building. I couldn't seem to get a deep breath. My lungs felt shallow, like they wouldn't let my body get enough air. Maybe I was getting too old for this job. I felt like I was at the start of a panic attack or that my knees would give out. Just then, Phil jumped out from behind a large palm. I screamed like I was the first one to die in a slasher film.

"Sorry, sorry, it's just me!" he said, both hands in the air. "I don't mean to keep scaring you!"

I struggled to regain composure. "What are you doing?" I pushed my teeth back in as quick as I could. They must've loosened with all the screaming.

"I just wanted to say great job today. Are you okay?" He came closer to me, and I instinctively backed away.

"Why'd you follow me?" I asked.

"I didn't!" He seemed genuinely hurt by my accusation. "I saw you coming so I was hiding here to surprise you. That was stupid, I'm sorry. Hug it out?"

I nodded then gave Phil a one-armed hug. I looked past him at the vacant parking lot. No one was there. He turned to see where I was looking.

"Was someone following you or something?" he asked.

I shook my head and put on my best smile. I even threw in some teeth. Phil put his arm around me.

"You don't look so good. How about we get you some electrolytes? I'll even admit to you where I live."

Phil took me to his apartment, which turned out to be on the seventh floor. 7G, to be precise. Who needed John's list of everyone's apartment numbers when I could just be invited in for Gatorade. His place had the same layout as mine, but was jam-packed with gym equipment and somehow cleaner-seeming. Right away, I was hit with the smell of lemon Pine Sol.

"Nice gym," I said as I sat down on his small gray couch.

Phil laughed as he poured me a tall glass of Gatorade. It was the turquoise flavor, probably something called Arctic Blast-Off or Glacier Shreds. It tasted a little like liquid plastic, but at least it was nice and cold.

He sat next to me, but the couch was so small our knees touched. I felt my face flush, and I set the glass down on the table. He swiftly lifted it to put a coaster underneath.

"Luella, what were you doing in the producers' building?"

"So, you were following me," I said.

He laughed. "Will you chill out? I saw you walking from that direction, that's all. But listen, if you want me to follow you, I can follow you. I just gotta clear my schedule." That damn dimple was out again.

"John showed me your picture," I said to him.

His brow furrowed. "Some people just won't let you forget your past. How'd you do it?"

"Do what?" I asked, taking another slow sip.

He stood and walked to the little kitchenette.

"I looked you up. I couldn't find anything from before four years ago. Pretty impressive."

"My life until four years ago was pretty uneventful," I said, nervously laughing. I finished my Gatorade and put the empty glass down on the coaster, like a proper lady. My stomach began growling again.

I really didn't have time for all this knee touching and cold Gatorade drinking. "I should go."

I stood and walked toward the door. Phil crossed the kitchenette to intercept me. He looked me in the eyes, then put his cool, dry hands on my shoulders.

"Hey. If my secret's safe with you, your secret's safe with me," he said.

I gave him a quizzical look. I wondered what secret of mine he thought he knew. Then I looked down at my watch. How was it already 4:45 p.m.? I turned to leave just as Phil went in for a kiss. His lips met my ear.

"Oh!" I said. "Sorry!"

"Whoops!" Phil laughed. "Well, let's just forget that ever happened."

He opened the door for me, and I darted out of his place like a bat out of hell.

Phil shouted after me, "Hey, did you get my flowers?"

I stopped running and turned around. "Those were from you?"

"Yeah." He smiled. "You like 'em?"

"Of course. Thank you." I smiled back.

So, Phil sent me those flowers. I guess that meant he knew where I lived. If I hadn't awkwardly dodged his kiss and run halfway down the hall, maybe things could have worked out between us. The bigger question was why was I crushing on a 20-something reality TV star? Why couldn't I just focus on the task at hand? I needed to get my head in the game. The time for food would have to come later. Off to George Striker's. Hopefully I'd get something out of him.

18

If you didn't already pick up on it, Luella is not the world's greatest detective. Often times, people just tell me things they're not supposed to, or they slip up. When I was working as a social worker, I'd listen to people say things they weren't supposed to all day long.

That's how I met Taylor Bell. He was a client. He started going to me with basic depression and anxiety symptoms, then all of a sudden his wife, Julia, disappeared. Every week, he'd come in and cry to me. At first I believed him. I'd listen to his grief and despondence as his social worker, Marie, then I'd put on a wig and go investigate his wife's disappearance as vigilante detective, Luella van Horn. For all my aspiring dual social worker-private detectives out there, just know this is considered a huge moral no-no.

I wanted to solve his problems. Was that so wrong? Well, yeah, in fact, it was. I do try to cut myself some slack — he was my first psychopath, after all.

I was the one who found her body in the Fresh Kills estuary. The police eventually found her ring finger buried in Bell's backyard, under the tulip bed. Taylor Bell was eventually sentenced to life in jail. For the love of all that is holy, I pray he does not make the connection that Marie and Luella are the same woman. Because if he did, he would probably find a way to kill me like he killed his wife.

I try not to dwell on the past, but I must've been reminiscing because I was hungry, and I was hungry because of these stupid teeth, and these stupid teeth were the reason I was in this mess in the first place. Walking to George Striker's place, I was in a piss-poor mood, to say the least. I hoped this meeting would be quick. I had big plans to get back to my apartment and eat a panini, a block of cheese, a bowl of popcorn, and a candy bar. Twix. No, Snickers. Snickers, for sure. I wondered if there was a way to incorporate gravy. Gravy sounded nice, too. Maybe I would dip the sandwich into the gravy. This meeting would need to be lightning fast. My stomach was audibly churning.

I arrived at George Striker's door at 5 p.m. on the dot. He lived in the only apartment on the top floor, which looked to be some sort of privilege. Before I could knock, George answered the door wearing a purple houndstooth silk robe.

"I heard the elevator go ding-ding!" He sounded like a drunk Mary Poppins.

I realized George Striker was the type of man who prided himself on never wearing a real shirt. I'd done some preliminary research on him. Before *Sex Island*, his only other directing work was on an indie movie called *Summer: Alone*, which seemed to be minimally successful in the festival circuit. After an extensive online search, I could only find the trailer, but luckily it felt just as long as the real movie. Black and white. Several shots of waves rushing over bare feet. Your typical pretentious garbage. I could see why Isa and he would get along, artistically speaking. And now he directed the last umpteenth seasons of a reality sex show. How did this fake British man get there?

George seemed happy to see me. And by happy, I mean drunk. As a reminder, it was only 5 p.m. "Come in, come in, come in," he slurred as he waved me inside.

I could smell the rum radiating off his skin. Once we were inside his apartment, I took a look around. All apartments were not created equal in this complex. His living room was about twice the size of mine, and there was a lofted area which looked to be where his bedroom was. I should also mention, the entire place was filled with trash. There were empty chip bags on the sofa, microwave dinner trays piled up on the coffee table, condom wrappers on the floor, a pile of crusty dishes in the sink. I noticed on the kitchen counter, he'd lit a candle. The place smelled like old garbage with a hint of vanilla.

He gestured to the living room. "'Scuse the mess. Want a drink?"

I said no, but Striker ignored me. He handed me a frosted tiki glass from the freezer and filled it to the brim with a white liquid from a blender.

"Cheers!" he said, clinking our glasses together.

"What is this?" I asked, taking a small sip. It was genuinely the most delicious thing I'd ever tasted.

"Coconut milk punch. My speciality." The way he said "speciality" gave it four extra syllables. The British accent was becoming more outlandish in his drunken state.

I took another sip, trying to remind myself not to drink so fast. Even if it tasted like a milkshake, it was a dangerous milkshake. I brushed a few old chip bags to the ground and sat down on the sofa.

"New guys coming tomorrow?" I asked him.

Striker toddled over to an armchair that faced the couch, sloshing half of his drink on the floor as he went. He sat and frowned.

"*Sex Island* hungry. Need more flesh," he said, making a claw with his empty hand. That was certainly an odd way of putting it.

I had so many questions for this man, but I didn't know where to start. My head was already starting to feel fuzzy. I wanted to know what his relationship was like with David G, and why he'd been working on this show for so long, and what was with that horrible fake accent. He was drunk enough where I knew if I asked the right questions, he would start talking and never stop. But if I asked a wrong one, he'd clam up and kick me out.

"You like the producers?" I probed, trying to stay casual.

He laughed at that. "Stephanie and John? Adore them! John's a putz and Stephanie's the craziest bitch I've ever met." He continued laughing to himself.

I figured as long as he was entertained, I could keep asking questions.

"You guys all friends?"

He laughed even harder then. "Friends?! That's rich!" He got up and refilled his glass in the kitchenette.

"So, not friends?" I called after him.

He burped loudly. "Stephanie and I have an understanding. I help her, she helps me, a-b-c, 1-2-3…"

Then he suddenly stopped speaking.

I looked over and saw he was standing in the kitchenette holding a large knife. Shit. If I was going to meet my maker, it would not be because of George fucking Striker. I scanned the surrounding garbage for something sharp and weapon-y, and the best I could come up with was an empty beer can. I quickly flattened it with my shoe to get the edges sharper.

I stood, readying myself for a fight. Was I drunk? I felt drunk. Then I saw George toss up a lime and fail to slice it midair. The lime fell to the ground and he followed suit, in a clatter of glassware and garbage. I rushed into the kitchenette to find him flat on his back, the knife still in his hand.

"Where'd the blimey lime go?" he asked me, looking from side to side. His landing robe placement was not ideal. I tried to avoid looking anywhere near his groin.

"Coulda killed yourself," I said as I tried to wrestle the knife from his hand. He held on tightly. I switched tactics. "High five!" I shouted. He dropped the knife and high-fived me. Thank you, coconut milk punch.

"C'mon! Up, up!" I lifted him to his feet, and he started laughing again.

His cell phone rang. He stood there, trying to fish it out of his robe pocket. He finally retrieved his phone and looked at the screen, then at me, then back at his screen. Suddenly, he seemed sober.

"Uh-oh. You gotta go!"

"Who was that?" I asked, feeling a bit unsteady on my own feet.

"Bye bye!" he shouted as he shuffled me over to the front door and yanked it open. I stumbled out, and he slammed the door shut behind me.

I stood in the hallway trying to get my bearings. I felt sick. My head was swimming, and my stomach was in knots. My hair hurt. I needed to get into bed. All I had to do was walk down the hall, then get on the elevator and push a button, then walk down another hall, and I'd be home. First step was to walk down this first hall. I took one step. Then I collapsed.

19

I woke up on a couch in a living room that was not my couch and not my living room. I patted myself down and felt relieved to still have all my clothes on. I did a loose inventory. Two arms: check. Two legs: check. No visible bleeding, though my left arm felt tender. Had I wet my pants? No. Had I thrown up? There did seem to be evidence of this, based on the bluish white puddle on the floor in front of me. I checked my teeth — those were somehow still in. Props to my beloved down-for-anything dentist, Dr. Frank! If you're ever in Staten Island and need a dentist, Dr. Michael Frank's your man. I reached up to check on the status of my wig, but it was gone. All that remained was my wig cap, still securely fastened to my head. Crap.

The apartment I was in was shaped like mine, but somehow smaller. The room around me was dark. Most of the light was coming from a small table lamp next to the couch. I could see there was also a light on in the bedroom. Slowly, I realized I was surrounded by mixed martial arts gear. Used hand wraps laid piled in a laundry basket. Boxing gloves hung from a hook on the wall. Was that a Bowflex next to the couch? There was a free-standing punching bag in the corner, and I spied a grappling dummy in the bedroom. Whatever was done to that thing in the bedroom, I didn't want to know.

I tried to sit up. Both my mouth and head felt fuzzy, and I could sense I wasn't done with the whole throwing-up phase. The room was spinning, so I focused all my attention on the grappling dummy. What's your name, I thought.

My name is Henry, and I'm a grappling dummy.

Hi Henry, I'm an undercover private detective and things are not going well for me. What's your deal?

I like boating, I'm gluten-intolerant, and I live in the bedroom because I'm the inanimate boyfriend of the person who lives here!

Well, nice to meet you, Henry.

My head drooped down to my chest, and I must've passed out again. Regaining consciousness later, I found myself in the same position, but this time my neck was stiff and the bedroom light had been turned off. I heard someone's key fob beeping at the door. I tried to stand, but that was not in the cards right now. If I was about to get beaten up by a mixed martial artist, it would certainly not be a fair fight. Goodbye, I told Henry. It's been fun.

Bye-bye, Luella!

The door opened slowly. The hallway was brighter than the apartment so the figure in the doorway was backlit. They were maybe 5'7". I could make out two long braids, a slim build. The figure stepped inside and I recognized her face. Isa.

"Hey, you're up," she said.

Was that a friendly tone? Concern in her voice? She was carrying several heavy bags. I only hoped they did not contain several heavy weapons. She dropped them on the counter and reached into the nearest one. "Gatorade?"

I shuddered to think of the stuff. The whole concept of Gatorade made me feel ill all over again. I knew it wasn't Gatorade's fault, the harmless colorful drink for active and hungover people alike. No, this was definitely the work of George Striker's coconut milk punch. Or more likely, the coconut milk punch with something else.

"What day is it?" I managed to ask.

"It's late Monday night, or early Tuesday morning, however you prefer to think about it."

"What?"

"It's 1 a.m.," Isa said.

"Water, please," I croaked.

TUESDAY

Isa filled up a glass from a Brita in the fridge. This broad was classy. She passed me the cool, filtered water, and I drank gratefully. I interpreted her kindness as a hopeful sign she wasn't going to kill me. Isa unpacked her bags, which turned out to contain groceries. Before I could set the glass down, I threw up the water. Who was the classy broad now?

"I'm so sorry," I told her.

I was shivering and sweating. There had to be a word in German that meant "more pathetic than pathetic," that would be absolutely perfect for my present circumstances.

"You're pretty sick," she said, wiping up my water-puke with a paper towel.

Isa draped another blanket over my shoulders and handed me a cup of ice. I took it with a shaky hand and put an ice cube in my mouth to water down the taste of bile.

"Let's see how you do with the ice, then maybe we'll graduate you to Saltines," she said.

"An incentive program," I said through the ice cube. I wanted to take my Luella teeth out so badly.

"You know, you're not the first person I've found passed out outside George Striker's apartment," she said, pulling up a chair across from me.

Isa brought out some knitting. It looked like she was about 75% done with an oversized, gray cardigan. Jeez, MMA, knitting, saving passed out people — how many hobbies did this woman have?

"Who else?" I asked.

"Oh, just about everybody. The last one on this couch was actually David G. If it makes you feel better, you don't look as bad as he did," she said, knitting away.

"How do you…?" I tried to continue but my Luella teeth were becoming impossible to talk through. I caught myself slurring.

"I live right below him, and I hear all," she said, finishing her row.

"You have my wig?" I asked.

"It's in the sink. I hope you have another one. It got pretty slimy." Isa walked to the sink and held up the wig. From this angle, it resembled a very wet, very dead lab rat.

Luckily, I'd packed three other wigs.

"I should go," I said. I tried to stand up but my legs shook so hard I had to sit down again. She looked up from her handiwork.

"Can I ask you something?"

I nodded.

"Are you who you say you are?" She squinted at me, like she'd already answered her own question.

"Are you?" I asked back.

"No," she answered straightforwardly, then resumed her knitting.

I needed to get back to my bed.

"Can I borrow a hat?" I asked. Isa didn't have one, so she lent me her MMA helmet. I popped it on, thanked her, and though it took me several minutes, managed to hobble out to the elevators. Isa was on eight. I pushed the down button, and eventually made it to my apartment on the fourth floor. I walked straight to the bed and lay face down, not bothering to even take off the helmet. Isa knew too much, but that wasn't necessarily a bad thing. That could be a very helpful thing indeed.

20

When I woke up again, it was Tuesday morning and I was still wearing the helmet. I smelled like hot trash. My head was pounding. I texted John to let him know I'd be taking the day off acting to focus on the investigation. He replied within seconds: *Do you have a lead???* I didn't respond.

I removed the teeth, shook out my hair, and took a long, hot shower to try to scrub off the previous day. From the air sex to being followed to the kiss mishap to the George Striker experience, I was just about done being Luella van Horn. I decided I would spend the day as Marie. If anyone stopped me, I would tell them I was Luella's secretary. Even though we share the same voice, eye color, face shape, and height, to my knowledge, no one has ever connected the dots. I'm telling you — sex appeal is the number one misdirect. If Elvis was walking around Memphis with frizzy brown hair and a chipped front tooth, he could be alive today and no one would recognize him.

It was 10 a.m. by the time I got myself to the shared pantry on the second floor for some dry toast and a room temperature 7Up. For the record, I prefer cold, but it did the trick.

I needed to learn more about George Striker. I knew he'd put something in my drink the night before. Maybe he gave the same thing to David G. Having a floor to himself, George certainly had opportunity. But what could the motive be? I figured I'd take the day to search George Striker's apartment. If there were drugs involved, I wanted to find them and take him down.

By 10:45 a.m., I made it up to the penthouse. Even if George Striker was very late to work, he still would've been on set for hours by then. My plan was simple: go to his apartment then call for housekeeping. I had a story all prepared. I would tell them I was planning to lose my virginity to George Striker that night and I needed to decorate his room with candles. You'd be surprised what people will do when you say your virginity is on the line. As Marie, I'm not the most unfortunate-looking woman, but people want to help out where they can.

I got to his door and dialed for housekeeping.

"Housekeeping and Maintenance," said a man with a gruff voice.

"Hi, I'm standing outside the penthouse apartment. I'm George Striker's girlfriend, and tonight I'm going to lose my virginity, and I was wondering if you could let me in to —" The gruff voice laughed at me and hung up. I might've been rusty — I blamed whatever was in the coconut milk punch.

Onto plan B, which was… just breaking in. The hallway ran east to west. I noticed there were security cameras on the far northeastern and southwestern corners of the hallway, though I doubted they were functional. The police had checked the seventh floor cameras the night David G's body was found, and it turned out they'd already been broken for a month. How convenient.

All the apartments in this complex operated on a key fob system, which meant no lock picking. The choices were A) hack into the main frame or B) knock down the door with my brute strength. I was hoping for A. On a whim, I tried my key fob on his door. To my utter shock, it clicked open.

The relief I felt at not having to physically bust down a door quickly faded. If my key fob opened his door, what did that mean for *my* door? What did that mean for *any* of the doors in this building? Is that how someone got David G's body into my bathtub?

In the sober light of day, George Striker's apartment looked even worse than it had the evening before. I nearly gagged at the smell. It was a delicate combination of rotten eggs, tomato paste (?), and Dolce and Gabbana Light Blue. How did he live like this?

I needed to stay focused. I was here to look for drugs. Most likely *Rohypnol*, or roofies, but I didn't want to narrow it down too quickly. In the kitchenette, I picked through what was left on the counter. Banana peels, a mostly empty Cup O Noodles, old takeout containers, a sticky blender. I found one bottle of pills under a McDonald's bag — the label said *Bupropion*. I recognized that as the generic name for the anti-depressant Wellbutrin. I looked at the big blue pills inside. Those were Bupropion alright. Sometimes being an ex-social worker had its perks.

I opened the fridge and then immediately closed the fridge. The mold stink hit me so hard, I almost stumbled backwards. I was beginning to think there was no way George Striker actually lived here. How was he not constantly physically ill? This seemed more like a staging area than anything else. Then on the couch, I saw the holy grail of private detective work. An open MacBook.

I pressed the spacebar with my knuckle. Right, of course it required a password. George Striker's password would be... something stupid. This guy lived in a constant state of being either drunk or hungover. It would be something easy to remember. Could it be as simple as *12345*? And... yes it could. I was actually in. This guy was a piece of work.

The joke was on me because immediately, porn began playing. Loudly. The thing about a paused porn video is, you know exactly when that person didn't need the porn anymore. I was getting nauseous again. On the screen, two women were collaborating on a joint blowjob for one man. Wow, George Striker was quite the gentleman, wasn't he?

I finally managed to close out the porn window, which caused three additional pop-up windows, because of course, George Striker didn't pay for porn. The man practically made porn and still, didn't see the value in his peers' work. Tsk, tsk, tsk.

There were two notifications on his Messages app. I clicked the green icon, carefully using the side of my knuckle. The first message was from Ethan at 7:11 a.m., and it was a photo of his erect penis. Yowza. Okay, maybe the ten-inch thing wasn't so far off. But why would Ethan send a dick pic to George so early in the morning? Were they involved? I guess I wouldn't put it past George Striker to abuse those power dynamics. The next message was from Stephanie, sent at 7:35 a.m. It said: *You get her?*

I'm no egomaniac, but I was pretty sure that *her* was me. I scrolled up for more context, and found a series of not exactly friendly texts, starting at 5:42 p.m. the night before. That must've been right around when he kicked me out.

Stephanie Hillson: You can't have Ethan

George Striker: You owe me

Stephanie Hillson: I don't owe you shit

George Striker: Why is she here

Stephanie Hillson: I told you why!

George Striker: I want Ethan

Stephanie Hillson: You get her?

Maybe Striker did a favor for Stephanie, as Stephanie now seemed to "owe" him. And Striker knew I was a private detective. He also wanted Ethan, and based on the photo, it looked like he was getting exactly what he wanted. But what kind of favor could Striker have done for Stephanie? Even if it didn't involve David G, I had a feeling it had something to do with me.

Detective work was kind of like camping, in that the major rule was "leave no trace." I read these messages and now they needed to be unread. That seemed simple enough. I looked through the menu of options — *File, Edit, View, Conversations* — apparently there was no way to unread a text on a MacBook. What the hell was Tim Cook thinking?

At this point, the whole avoid-leaving-fingerprints thing had gone out the window. I was in a full-blown panic. I clicked on *Conversations* again. I scrolled through the choices — *Block Person, FaceTime Video, FaceTime Audio* — and that is when I accidentally clicked *FaceTime Audio*. I was now somehow calling Stephanie.

They say there are two main reactions to a stressful situation: fight and flight. I can promise you there's a third, and it's staying put and muttering "oh no" over and over again.

"Oh no, oh no, oh no," I muttered over and over again. My brain went blank. All of the blood in my body rushed to my face. Of course, she picked up on the first ring.

"What do you want, Striker?" She sounded like she was walking, and fast. I tried not to make a sound. My shallow breathing was being picked up by the microphone. Freakin' Tim Cook made a hyper-sensitive microphone but no way to unread a text? That's practically immoral!

I focused all of my remaining brain power on my hand. *Hang up*, I thought. *Hang up!* I felt like I was moving under water as I placed my finger on the mousepad and moved the arrow to the red button that would end the call.

She was pissed now. "Striker, what the hell is going —" Finally I hung up. I closed the laptop and ran out of there. George Striker would likely know someone had been in his apartment, but I hoped he wouldn't know it was me. From what it seemed, he had a healthy amount of enemies here.

21

I was shaking as I took the elevator down to the seventh floor. Now that I knew what my key fob was capable of on the penthouse, I wondered what else it could open for me. I knew David G had lived on seven — John's list said his apartment was 7A. I walked down to the end of the hall and took a long look at his door.

Sometimes when you're solving a murder case, it's easy to get lost in the nitty-gritty of the crime, the suspects, the clues. One can quickly forget about the victim, who had family and friends and a whole life ahead of him. It all hit me, looking at David G's apartment door. Just over a week ago, he'd been alive, living in this apartment, coming and going through this very door. I suddenly felt so sad, I didn't know if I could handle going inside. I hoped my key fob wouldn't work.

I swiped it in front of the detector, and the door clicked open. So much for high-tech security. What was the point of anyone closing their doors around here? Right away, the room smelled like musky cologne and unwashed gym clothes. Boy smells. His place was tidy, for the most part. An inside-out sweatshirt was laid over a chair in the living room. There was a dirty bowl and spoon in the sink. Someone had cleaned out the fridge, thankfully. In the cabinet, all that was left was an open box of Cheerios and a mostly full container of PG Tips black tea. Seemed a little British for a 21-year-old from Philadelphia. My mind went to Striker.

I got an eerie feeling standing there, like at any moment the ghost of David G might walk in and tell me to get the hell out of his place. I really wanted to leave. But I didn't know when I'd find myself back there, so I figured it would be best to be thorough. Cautiously I made my way into the bedroom.

His bed was made. His clothes still hung in the closet. A framed photo of his family sat on top of his dresser. David G must have been fifteen years old in it. There he was, with his mother, his father, his older sister, and a guy with his arms wrapped around the older sister's waist. The guy seemed to be in his early 20s. I looked closer and immediately recognized those blue eyes. John. He looked like he was practically a member of the family. Why would he downplay their closeness the last time we spoke?

I took a photo of the family picture, then wandered into David G's bathroom. There was a half-squeezed tube of toothpaste on the counter. His toothbrush was still in its holder. It made my heart sink. I felt the bristles and quickly pulled my hand away. It was wet. Whoa. *Why* was it *wet*?

If David G was the last person to use this toothbrush, it certainly would have been dry by now. He went missing over a week ago. Someone else had been in there. And that someone had used a dead man's toothbrush. I became quite cold and found my hands wouldn't stop shaking. I needed to get out of there.

I ran down the seventh floor hallway and pushed the down button for the elevator about nineteen times. *C'mon, c'mon, c'mon.* Finally, the doors opened, and my breath caught in my chest. There, in the elevator, stood George fucking Striker. I swallowed my scream.

"I'll get the next one," I said, my voice trembling. He'd seen me in his place. He was coming to get me.

"Whatever," he said, barely looking at me. There was no checking me out. There was no British accent. The elevator doors closed. It hit me — George Striker did not recognize me as Marie. Without the wig and the teeth, he had no interest in me at all. I rushed to the stairs and promptly threw up my toast and 7Up.

Standing in the empty stairwell, I did some hasty mental math. If George was in the elevator going down, that meant he was coming from above. So, either from the eighth floor or the penthouse. He couldn't have been coming from the penthouse — surely I would have seen him. Or heard him. Could he have been hiding in a closet? Did I check the closets? If he had seen me searching through his computer, he would have recognized me in the elevator. So, if he wasn't coming from the penthouse, he must've been coming from eight. The only two people who lived on eight were Isa and Ethan, and I had foolishly assumed they were both on set.

22

When I got back to my apartment, I decided I needed to lie face-down on the couch for a while. In theory, this sounded wonderful. In practice, the couch smelled remarkably like the asses of the previous tenants, so I sat up and found myself brushing strange crumbs off my forehead. Upon closer inspection, they appeared to be Dorito remains. I'd never eaten Doritos on this couch. They must've been a previous tenant's Doritos. This apartment building officially sucked.

In the before-times of anxious restlessness, I would have watched an episode of *Sex Island* to feel better. But now that I was on the show, the magic was completely gone. David G's murder may have also tainted it for me, who's to say, really.

But as if I was on autopilot, I turned on another episode — from the Monday before I arrived — and half-watched as Sarah and Tasha got into a screaming match about dog legs. Sarah was screaming that dogs had four legs, while Tasha insisted dogs had two legs and two arms. It barely registered that Sarah wasn't acting nice for once.

My mind felt like it was on a demonic merry-go-round. There were just too many suspects — Stephanie, George Striker, Ethan, Tasha, John, Isa, and the list went on and on. I wondered — was it normal in show business for everyone to seem capable of murder? How did this business even function on a day-to-day basis?

I knew I needed to narrow down this list. I had a theory but it didn't hold much water if there was no confession, no evidence, no nothing. I was starting to give myself a hard time, which doesn't help anyone, so I decided to take a long bath. I set my Luella teeth in a cleaning solution, brushed my backup wigs, and ordered takeout from a place called *Beetle Bob's* that specialized in something called a "wet potato." From the photos, it looked like a baked potato covered in chili. I really hoped it was chili. The last thing I needed that evening was someone delivering me a baked potato with a steaming hot turd on top of it.

Forty-five minutes later, the doorbell rang. My wet potato, come to Mama! I answered the door wearing a robe and a towel wrapped around my head. The delivery guy handed me a greasy paper bag that was heavier than it looked, and I tipped him in cash. In my experience, that was when delivery guys typically walked away. But he remained standing in the doorway patting down his pockets. He was wearing blue cargo shorts, which gave him quite a lot of pockets to pat down.

"Can I help you?" I asked him, trying my best not to sound passive-aggressive.

"Um, one sec," he said. The delivery guy had finally found what he was looking for. Pulling out a black envelope from his back pocket, he looked at me sheepishly. It was the same type of black envelope I'd seen in the mailroom. Same thickness. Same size.

"Someone told me to give this to you," he said.

"Who?" I asked.

"Don't know," he said, averting his eyes. He had to know who.

I gave him another $20. "Who!" I demanded.

He looked to either side. "Some guy. He was wearing a jacket with the hood up, so I couldn't really see his face."

I felt blood rushing to my head, and suddenly my robe felt too hot.

"How'd he know you were coming to my apartment?" I asked.

The delivery guy started talking faster now. "He was just hanging out in the lobby, and I asked him where the elevators were. He asked me where I was heading, so I told him your apartment number. I didn't give him your name or anything! Beetle Bob's does not give away names! Listen, I got a bunch of other deliveries to make. Can I go?"

I was sweating all over. "Sure. Go."

I shut the door and plopped the wet potato on the counter. I put the envelope on top of the refrigerator. I told myself not to read it until I had eaten something, because if I read it first, I would not be in the mood to eat at all.

I ate my wet potato slowly, not taking my eyes off the top of the refrigerator. It turned out the wet part was some combination of lentils, two kinds of cheese, avocado, and a garlicky, green sauce, all on top of a baked potato the size of a kids' football. I didn't mind the taste, but it felt like the kind of food one stopped being able to properly digest after age 25.

I finished eating and wiped my mouth on a paper napkin. It was time to read whatever was in that envelope. I grabbed it from the top of the fridge and laid it on the counter. Just like last time, *Marie* was written in neat, white lettering across the front. Same handwriting as before, no address. I figured fingerprints were a lost cause with the delivery guy's hands all over it, so I opened it quickly, carelessly. Inside, there was a small black card. In block white writing, it said:

Anyone get poisoned back in Staten Island?

My stomach flipped. Staten Island was a deep cut. Too deep. I had the nagging fear Taylor Bell was somehow involved in this. Last I checked he was still in prison, but I learned to never underestimate what he was capable of.

I didn't sleep more than two hours that night.

WEDNESDAY

That morning, I woke up at 5 a.m. without an alarm. I had missed three vaguely threatening texts from John:

You'll be on set today?

See you on set today.

Can you confirm I'll see you on set today.

The period at the end of that third text was unsettling, to say the least.

Isa arrived at my door at 6 a.m., and I was ready to go. It seemed both of us had made a silent pact not to discuss what happened Monday night, just to carry on as usual. I was fine with that. My backup wig had been braided into pigtails for a previous undercover gig (a sting on a gymnastics coach... need I say why), so I left them in. Isa also had her hair in braided pigtails.

"Look at us, twinning!" she said, high-fiving me. Isa seemed giddy. She practically galloped to set.

"You're gonna meet the new guys today! There's two of them, and they are both very fine, if I may say so myself," Isa said, shimmying her shoulders. If this was the work of psychiatric medication, I intended to try whatever she was on.

"Oh great," I said, lightly jogging to keep up with her.

"You know what? One of them is from New York! What's the borough you're from again?"

"Manhattan. Why?" I asked.

"Oh, okay, this guy is from Staten Island. Is that far from you?"

Not far at all.

23

They occasionally did this thing on *Sex Island* called *Women's Choice Wednesday*, where the female contestants chose a sex partner first thing in the morning. By that evening, the women had to decide whether they would stay with that sex partner or move on. This usually happened on a Wednesday when the men outnumbered the women. The men who weren't selected in the morning only got to stay on the show if a woman decided to move on from the sex partner she initially chose. If everyone opted to stay with the men they'd first picked, that morning's rejects went home, forfeiting the $100,000 prize.

I've seen the most confident, symmetrical faces crumble in those moments. It's almost heartbreaking, but then you remember that you've been totally complicit for watching it, and the "rejects" would likely get a generous brand sponsorship after this was all over.

Isa brought me to my trailer. This time, I ordered the protein waffles.

"I didn't know you knew about the protein waffles," she said with a smile, jotting something down on her clipboard.

"I hear things," I said. She nodded conspiratorially. I couldn't tell if we were still talking about the waffles.

She left me to change into my wardrobe, which I was relieved to see was a full-length maxi dress. I couldn't believe my eyes. What had I done to deserve so much fabric! I tried it on — the front was loose and, dare I say, flattering! But then I felt a light breeze behind me. I turned around, and there, out in the open, was my wide, flat ass.

The dress stopped at my lower back. Was this a cruel trick? Was this fashion? Who would make a dress that exposed the entire ass?! Then I saw, also on the hanger, hung a rhinestoned g-string thong. I was to wear the g-string *with* the dress. For *rhinestoned modesty*. I decided then and there that even if I found the killer, I would still do everything in my power to send the wardrobe ladies to jail.

An hour later, the entire cast was brought to the *Cuddle Puddle*. If you've never seen the show, the *Cuddle Puddle* is basically a pile of Home Goods throw pillows where the cast members go to lose their self-esteem. It's usually surrounded by lit tiki torches even though the show is mostly filmed in broad daylight.

The idea is to basically lock eyes with someone on the *Cuddle Puddle*, then walk hand-in-hand to your cabana to consummate what started on the *Cuddle Puddle*. *Cuddle Puddle, Women's Choice Wednesday*... I know it's a lot. But these producers had to broadcast an hour-long reality show every night. Even the bad ideas made it to air.

We were all placed in a circle and propped up on the Home Goods cushions. It was wild to see how even the stars of these shows were basically treated like set pieces with a pulse. A production assistant sat me between Blair and Sarah, directly across from Phil. Phil smiled at me, and I managed to smile back. I still felt a lingering awkwardness from our ear kiss, and I wondered if he did, too. Between David N and Nate were two empty cushions. I assumed these were designated for the new guys.

Once we were situated, George Striker waltzed onto set. I felt my blood boil. This morning he was wearing an actual T-shirt but it had fashion rips in it, exposing not one but both of his nipples. It was a shirt seemingly designed to punish the people around him. He walked around the *Cuddle Puddle* assessing camera angles and slightly tripped on a cushion, which brought me more joy than I anticipated.

He addressed the cast. "Alright children, we're going to meet two new hunky-hunks today, so be on your best—or naughtiest—behavior."

Sarah smiled at Blair. David N noticed, and at that moment, he looked like a birthday boy with a popped balloon. By then, he'd been paired with Sarah for at least eight episodes.

George continued, "It's *Women's Choice Wednesday*, so once we meet the two new boys, our girlies will pick their partners, and off you'll go!"

The way he kept referring to us as "children" and "boys" and "girls" — something was very wrong with this man. He called, "Action!" then scurried off to the shaded video village where he sat with the producers watching the proceedings. In his absence, Isa stayed on set, yelling out instructions she received through her ear piece.

"Sarah look to David N. And Blair, lick your lips and look at Nate. Okay, Blair, we had a camera issue, please lick your lips again. Tasha, wave to Ethan. Hold. Ethan, blow a kiss to Luella. And Luella, look to Phil."

I looked to Phil, and he was earnestly looking back at me. I guessed that meant Striker and the producers wanted me to choose Phil. Copy that. Then the new guys were trotted in like two prized horses in a big parade.

The first guy to walk out was tall and muscular with short, curly hair. I overheard him introduce himself to camera.

"My name's Justin, I'm 20 years old, and I'm a model-slash-actor-slash-model consultant."

A model… consultant. Sounded like a legitimate stream of income to me!

The second guy to walk out was more compact. I couldn't make out his face since he was talking to a camera across from me. He looked to be about 5'8" which was short for the show, and he wore a flat-brimmed New York Jets hat. He wore two gold chains, he was shirtless, and his back was covered in one large tattoo of an eagle, mid-flight. I mean, this guy just screamed Staten Island.

He turned to face the *Cuddle Puddle*, and I was shocked to recognize him. Baby AJ! I'm sure he didn't go by "Baby" anymore, but he did back when I knew him. He was my best friend Lauren's younger cousin. I practically grew up with this kid. I could not believe he was here.

Lauren was the only friend I'd told about Luella, and long story short, she didn't take it well. She thought I was making a huge mistake with my life. We hadn't spoken in years. Seeing AJ now, I remembered how we used to take turns pushing him down Lauren's stairs in a laundry basket, how he'd giggle and scream. He was such a funny little kid. But that was all over a decade ago.

Isa spoke again. "Luella, your jaw is open in a weird way. The producers are asking if you can close your jaw?"

I closed my jaw. AJ looked at me then, and I watched in real-time as he put the pieces together. Here was his cousin's friend, Marie, wearing a blonde wig and fake teeth. I know I said no one's ever realized Marie and Luella are the same person, but I guess that excludes people who have known me since childhood. He gave me a tentative wave. I waved back.

Hannah, the makeup lady, sidled over and whispered in my ear. "Honey, you're bright red! Mind if I powder you back to normal?"

I nodded while my mind raced. How could I get AJ to not blow my cover here?

"We don't get those rock 'n' roll types around here too often, do we?" Hannah whispered about an inch from my face. "I say go for it, babe. His booty looks like a juicy peach, and I'd like to bite right into it, feel it drip down my chin."

Everyone here was unapologetically inappropriate. I blamed the sun.

Isa announced that it was time to pick our partners. The women took turns choosing. Sarah chose David N, who was visibly relieved, and off they went to a private cabana. Blair chose Nate. Then to everyone's surprise, Tasha chose the new guy, Justin. Ethan punched a Home Goods cushion then sulked off, kicking sand at the cameras that followed him. If I were still a licensed social worker, I might have diagnosed Ethan with Intermittent Explosive Disorder, a condition where the angry outbursts are disproportionate to the circumstances. It's a fun one.

It was time for me to choose my partner for the day. I needed to talk to AJ alone, and this was my chance. Phil would understand.

"I choose AJ," I said.

AJ smiled, and we crawled toward each other in the *Cuddle Puddle*.

"Hi!" I said.

He hugged me. "Hi! I can't believe you're here! This is so great!"

"C'mon, let's go," I said, hoping that I could cut off the conversation before he called me Marie on camera.

I remembered only then that I was wearing a butt-less dress, and I had been crawling on my hands and knees. Knowing the producers, I would bet my life that they aimed a camera directly into my rhinestoned asshole. AJ helped me up, and it was then I saw Phil's face. He didn't look angry, per se, more just confused. I tried to make eye contact, but he kept his eyes on the ground in front of him.

"Sorry, Phil." I said, startling him. Phil looked up.

"Huh? Oh, it's fine! Have fun." He went back to looking at that same spot on the ground.

AJ took my hand and we walked toward the only open cabana. I couldn't help but feel a little guilty. At the end of the night, if everyone stayed with their chosen partners, Ethan and Phil would be sent home.

24

We got to the cabana and the two cameramen positioned themselves around the bed. Today, one of them smelled like cheap marijuana. The sound guy put out his cigarette in the sand and coughed out, "Sound rolling!" The shorter of the two cameramen yelled, "Action!"

AJ and I awkwardly sat next to each other on the bed. He asked if I wanted a massage, and I said, "Sure." It would buy me some time. I needed to figure out how to tell him I was Luella van Horn now, without also being picked up by the microphones. I turned around, and he started rubbing my shoulders. I realized from the way I was sitting, the top part of my ass was just out there, facing AJ like a friendly dog. Damn, I really hated this dress. I prayed I wouldn't fart. I cursed Beetle Bob and his wet potato.

AJ suddenly stopped massaging me, so I turned back around to face him. He closed his eyes and brought his lips closer to my face. I let him kiss me. His lips were lank and cold, and I could feel his stubble on my chin. There was a sibling-like quality to the kiss that made me recoil. Everything felt wrong. I couldn't kiss Baby AJ — he was Baby AJ!

"Get under the covers," I insisted.

He nodded his head vigorously and dove under the sheets head-first like a dolphin. Was he actually into this? I was appalled, hoping he was just an incredible actor. I lifted the top sheet and found him under there, already naked, lying on his side like a fetus. Truly, ultrasound vibes.

"Hi," he cooed.

I winced. No cooing. No cooing!

"I can't believe this is finally happening," he continued. "You and me. AJ and Marie, at last."

"I need to talk to you!" I said in my sternest whisper. I let out a loud fake moan and humped the air. AJ's eyes went wide. He growled then took me in his arms. I squirmed away and let out another fake moan. He traced his finger around my face.

"Okay, you're my babysitter, and I'm…"

"Shut up!" I whispered.

"No, you shut up…" He was batting at me like a playful cat. At that moment, I wished I would fart.

"Put your clothes on!" I mouthed.

"Marie, what's wrong? Are you mad at me or something?" he asked, wiggling back into his boxer briefs.

"Not mad!" I mouthed.

"Marie, it's so crazy we're both here," he mouthed back.

I got very close to his ear. "Not Marie. Luella."

He nodded his head to suggest he was starting to get it. "Okay. *Luella* then." He winked at me and licked his lips, which meant he was not getting it at all.

"I need to talk to you." I was speaking so quietly into his ear, I hoped he could still hear me.

Just then, I was prodded twice in the back of the leg. I pulled the duvet cover down, and found the sound guy tapping both of us with his boom mic.

"Producers say they can't hear what you two are saying. Gotta speak up." An unlit cigarette dangled precariously from his lips.

"Sorry about that!" I yelled at a volume I hoped would hurt someone wearing headphones back in video village. I pulled the covers over us again and looked at AJ.

I mouthed, "Meet me at 5 p.m. My room, 4E."

"For sex?" he mouthed. His eyes were so earnest, I wanted to die.

I shook my head and rolled my eyes at the same time. My own version of multi-tasking.

From under the covers, I heard a muffled woman's voice say, "Let's take five."

When I pulled them down, I saw that the cameramen and sound guy were gone, and Stephanie was standing there with her hands on her hips. She didn't look happy.

"Hey AJ, I'm Stephanie, one of the executive producers here. Welcome to *Sex Island!* Wanna have a chat?"

She was already heading out of the cabana curtain doors before AJ was out of bed. He stood up and scrambled after her, yanking up his shorts and straightening his Jets hat as he walked. I watched as she took him arm-in-arm, and they made their way toward the shore together.

Why on earth was AJ here? Some part of me feared he was walking directly into the spider's web.

25

Ten minutes later, Isa found me drinking an off-brand energy drink at the crafty table. She let me know the producers had given me the rest of the day off, and they suggested I use it to "tan my buttocks." These people were just endlessly rude.

I stopped by my trailer to grab a robe, my phone, and my key fob, then wandered back out toward the beach. It was almost lunch, and I decided it was time to pay another visit to Tasha. I really wanted to cross her off my suspect list, but first I needed to know more about what had been going on with her and David G in the days before he died.

When I got to Tasha's cabana, she and Justin were still going at it. From the sound of it, they were hopefully close to being done. I stood outside the door digging my toes in the sand, when it occurred to me that the last time I saw AJ, he was still in middle school. I was getting the heebie-jeebies. It'd been years since Lauren and I had spoken, but I texted her anyways.

I saw your cousin on Sex Island!

She didn't respond. I immediately followed up.

It's been too long! It's Marie btw

Still nothing. I switched tactics.

So, are you gonna watch your cousin and me have sex on TV lol lol lol lol

Finally, I saw the three dots appear. She replied:

Just stay out of my life.

A lesson on why some stones are best left unturned. I put my phone away just as Tasha walked out of her cabana barefoot, carrying strappy sandals over her shoulder with one hooked finger. She walked fast, and I jogged to catch up to her.

"Tasha!" I yelled. I was already out of breath. Finally, she stopped walking.

"What do you want? I have to pee or I'll get a UTI."

"I need your advice," I managed to get out between wheezes.

She looked me over. "Okay, come with me to the bathroom." She resumed her quick pace, and I tried my best to keep in stride.

The cast bathroom was located inside the lobby of a nearby air-conditioned building used mostly for crew housing. It was surprisingly very beautiful in there. The tiled floor was ivory and lavender and the mirrors had little flowers engraved on the glass. The three toilets were lavender, too.

It was someone's job (probably Isa's) to supply the bathroom with a basket of sundries, and there on the sink was everything you could possibly need: stain remover, mouthwash, dental floss, hairspray, hand lotion, gum. I helped myself to a piece of blotting paper, put it to my forehead, and immediately felt ill by the amount of grease I'd removed. Tasha went into the middle stall to pee. The right stall was also occupied, but I couldn't tell who it was from their legs.

"So, what do you need my advice about?" Tasha asked, audibly peeing.

"Break ups," I said, trying to remain casual.

"Uh-oh. You and Phil not doing so good? That's gonna be a shit show."

The toilet flushed. She walked out of the stall and stepped up to the sink. In the stall next to her, the mystery person's legs still hadn't moved.

"How'd you dump David G?" I asked, looking at Tasha through the mirror. She looked at herself. She washed her hands, then shook them dry.

"Well, he was secretly sleeping with, like, a ton of people at the time, which is not allowed. That's, like, the one rule of this show. You have to be upfront. That's the only way it works."

I nodded at her reflection. "Who else?" I asked.

She rifled through the basket until she found hairspray. She popped open the small can and sprayed it all over her head. I tried not to inhale.

"I don't know, I feel like something was going on with Blair, and he was always on-again-off-again with Sarah, and I swear there was something between him and George Striker."

"What about Stephanie?" I asked.

She scrunched up her button nose. "Ew, no way. She's old. That's gross."

The funny thing about agism is nobody realizes they'll be old one day, too. And only if they're lucky.

"How'd you leave things?" I asked, digging through the basket for some chapstick.

We locked eyes in the mirror. She briefly cocked her head to one side before speaking.

"Look, we're all sad about David G, but at some point, we have to move on, right?"

There was a hostility in her voice that hadn't been there before.

"What happened with you and Ethan?" I asked.

"Bitch, you ask a lot of questions. You're really better off not knowing too much around here," she said.

She turned on her heels and walked out. The door slammed behind her, and the bang echoed in the tiled bathroom. I wondered what, specifically, set her off. Then I heard another toilet flush. The stall door swung open. Standing there was the sound guy.

26

The sound guy's face turned a bright shade of pink.

"Shit. I thought you left with the other girl." He made his way to the sink but didn't wash his hands. Instead he picked through the basket for a pack of spearmint gum, which he pocketed.

"What's your name?" I asked as I vigorously washed my hands, hoping I could lead by example. He didn't follow.

"I'm Max. You're Luella, right?" He extended his filthy hand to shake mine, and I left him hanging.

"Okay, then! See ya, princess!" he said, holding up both hands as if in surrender.

With that, he walked out of the bathroom. I followed him as he exited the building. The early-afternoon sun was almost at its highest and the humidity was thicker than usual. I would have described that Wednesday's forecast as *minestrone*. The ocean waves crashed hard against the shore, drowning out all other noise. I had to shout to Max to be heard.

"Wait!" I said. He stopped and looked at me. I continued, "This David G stuff... I'm scared." I tried pouting my lips but it didn't matter. He was very clearly staring at my breasts.

"Freaky, I know," he said, nodding.

"You must hear a lot," I said, gesturing to the headphones hanging around his neck.

"Well, I hear a lot more than people would like to think." He pulled out a cigarette and lit it.

"Like what?"

He took a long drag then looked around. "I got a good sense of what happened to David G."

"What's your sense?" I asked.

"Why don't you tell me what you're doing here first?" He took another drag.

"What do you mean?" I started to panic. Was this the guy who'd been sending me the black envelopes?

"You're probably ten years older than everybody else. No offense, but you're maybe a six or a seven, while all these other chicks are tens."

So Max wasn't the kindest man I'd ever met, but at least I could rule out that he knew my secret identity. Maybe his no-filter approach could prove to be useful.

"What are you doing on this show?" he asked.

People tend to go on these shows for one of three reasons: they want to be famous, they already are famous, or they used to be famous. I decided, based on my age, it would be most believable to go with door number three.

"I used to be famous," I said.

Hearing that, Max softened. "Ohhh, I thought you maybe looked familiar. What were you in?"

"Um… commercials? And porn." I really should have left it at commercials. This guy looked like he ate, slept, and breathed porn.

"Yeah, I've definitely seen you! Awesome." He high-fived me then. It was too fast to dodge. If I soon developed pink eye, I'd know Max was the culprit.

"Awesome," I said.

"But yeah, that David G stuff is crazy. He was missing for days before they even called the police. Fucked up. And everyone knows who did it, but they won't report him."

"Totally..." I waited for him to say something, but he was too busy trying to blow a smoke ring. "Who's *him*?" I eventually asked.

"Ethan! Dude's got anger issues for real. On my tapes, I got legit recordings of him saying he was gonna kill David G. That botched Tasha alliance totally messed him up. And everyone knew David G was gonna win this thing. Dude was so good at sex. Trust me. I hear all."

He smirked, then smashed the butt of his cigarette into the sand with the toe of his flip-flop.

"You know, Ethan used to live on seven but he kept getting into fights with Nate once David G went missing, so they moved him up to eight," he continued. "Real geniuses running this place. Like Ethan can't go down a floor if he wants to beat the shit out of Nate."

"Right," I said.

"Oh, and that ten-inch rumor is total bullshit," Max chuckled to himself. "Hey what's one of your movies called? I wanna check it out. I'm a big supporter of the pornographic arts."

I pretended I couldn't hear him, what with the waves and all. He began to shout-repeat his question when I said I had to go.

"I'll keep an eye out for ya!" he yelled after me as I walked away.

For all the creepy vibes, Max did have access to a lot of information. I wondered if he was right about Ethan.

27

Everyone was on lunch for the next hour, so I figured nobody would miss me if I snuck off to the police department. I wanted concrete information, and I had the sense both Stephanie and John were withholding evidence.

John wasn't telling me the full extent of his relationship with David G, and Stephanie's *did you get her* text still wasn't sitting right with me. I set out on foot, assuming it was a small enough island. From my phone, it looked like the police station was about three miles away. I lived in New York, I could handle a three mile walk.

As it turned out, I could not handle a three mile walk. What the map on my phone didn't tell me was that many streets on the island were dead-ends, which required one to either double back or practically scale a wall. It was also sweltering outside. The further I walked from the ocean, the stiller the air became. I finally arrived at the police department wilted like an old carnation. The very kind receptionist asked if I needed to go to the hospital. I said, "No, thank you."

I asked to speak with Detective Johannes or Detective Sandro, whoever was working that day. The receptionist told me Detective Johannes was on duty, but he was at lunch. She looked at the big clock on the wall.

"He should be back soon if you'd like to wait."

There was a water cooler in the corner of the room with a bunch of small paper envelopes resting on top. I finally figured out these things were cups, and disintegrated six of them trying to drink about a gallon of water. I took a seat in a hard plastic chair and picked up a children's magazine about carrots. I read a fascinating article about rabbit food — apparently it's not just carrots, it's also arugula. By the time Detective Johannes got back from lunch, I was convinced I should retire from private detective work and open my own rabbit farm.

Detective Johannes still had that spectacular mustache. He recognized me from the night David G was found, and quickly ushered me back to his office.

Johannes' office was small with dark wooden furniture. The walls, once painted tan, could have benefited from a fresh coat. Toward the ceiling, there were long, windy cracks, probably due to the salty air or the humidity or both. Johannes' desk was piled high with files and papers. This felt like the kind of place where a case could turn cold and fast. I sat across from him in an old wooden chair that creaked whenever I shifted in it. Someone had tried to make it more homey with a dusty blue seat cushion. There were tiny daisies embroidered around its edges. I doubted this was Detective Johannes' touch.

He tucked a few loose files into the metal cabinet behind him.

"So, what can I do for you? It was your apartment, right? Let's see…" He picked up a file and began reading. "7E? You're a cast member on the show, yes?"

"I'm actually working the case."

"Ah! A private detective! What, those Hollywood types don't trust the island's police?" He laughed cynically.

"They wanted it kept quiet," I said.

"I see." He leaned forward in his chair and twisted his mustache. "So you want my help?"

I nodded. He stared into the middle distance for a moment, then made direct eye contact.

"How about we help each other?"

I leaned forward, too, and the old chair whined. "Fair," I said.

"I want this case solved. That TV show is a big source of revenue for the island, and if it goes unsolved, they will probably blame it on some local. Then they'll move production to some other island, and all those taxes they pay will go with them. I don't want that. My boss, the mayor, doesn't want that, either. What happened to that kid is very unfortunate, but as you can see, I'm a little overwhelmed with my other caseloads at the moment." He gestured to the piles. "So, how about I tell you what we know, then you go do some snooping or whatever it is you do, and you come back and tell me what you've learned. Is it a deal?"

He held out his hand. I shook it.

"So, what do you know?" I asked.

"Let's see." He scanned through the file and began to read aloud.

"Cause of death was kidney failure. There was a significant amount of ethylene glycol in his system. No fingerprints found on the body." He looked up at me. "Looks like you need to find someone who has access to antifreeze. And that narrows it down to... just about everybody." He chuckled to himself and tossed the file across the desk.

"Sorry it's not much. Enjoy your reading."

I caught it and tucked it under my arm.

"I will."

It was disheartening to learn the police didn't know much more than I did, but at least the producers weren't actively colluding against me. I stood up and navigated my way out of the cramped office. I was almost out the door when Johannes stopped me.

"Luella, something I just remembered. We had a case here with antifreeze once. A woman killed her husband. The thing was, the woman didn't give it to him all at once. It was small amounts over time. Some in his salad dressing one week, some in his drink the next, then some in the steak sauce, some in the gravy. Eventually, the guy falls down dead. That one was tough to solve."

"How'd you do it?" I asked.

He chuckled again. "She turned herself in. If I were you, I'd look at the wife."

28

I walked out of the police station thinking about Tasha and was immediately hit with a wall of humidity so thick, I couldn't breathe. In these conditions, I just couldn't face the long, winding walk back to the apartment. I thought of my options and decided to call John. He picked me up fifteen minutes later in the white 12-passenger van.

"How'd you even get here? Did Isa drive you?" John asked as I swung open the side door and hurled myself into the back row. I had the feeling I smelled like absolute shit.

"I walked," I replied.

"Seriously? Luella, there are so many winding streets on this island. It must've taken you an hour, at least."

"An hour forty-five," I said.

John craned his neck around. "C'mon, don't be way in the back like that. I drove all the way here, the least you can do is sit up front with me."

I reluctantly navigated myself up to the front of the van, hoping the air conditioner vents going full-blast would help dilute my body funk.

"You missed the afternoon elimination. We had Sarah say you had an allergic reaction to latex. That that's why you weren't there."

"Who got eliminated?" I asked.

"Well, it was quite the episode. Tasha dumped Justin for Phil, and since you weren't there to choose, AJ got to stay. Luckily for Ethan, he had immunity from a previous week. That new guy, Justin, is going home already."

"Too bad," I said.

"Yeah, well, that's *Sex Island* for ya!" He was quiet for a beat while he drummed on the steering wheel.

"You want to get some ice cream?" he asked, forcing a smile.

"Okay, Dad," I said, buckling my seatbelt. John rolled his eyes as he sped down a side street.

He drove us deeper into the island's mainland. We didn't say much to each other on the ride, but the further I got from set, the better I felt. I could sense John's mood lightening, too. We eventually stopped at a small ice cream shop called *Scoopy's*. Their logo was a knock-off Snoopy holding a melting popsicle in one paw and giving a thumbs up with the other. I had high hopes for the place.

We stepped up to the service window. I ordered a strawberry milkshake, and John got a chocolate one. He treated. The heat was oppressive, so we sipped them in the comfort of the air-conditioned van. I couldn't speak for John's, but mine tasted like magic.

We were both loudly slurping up the dregs of our milkshakes when he broke the silence with a question.

"So. What'd you find out at the police station?"

I sucked up my last sip. "Nothing new."

He nodded. "David G's sister is coming to town on Friday. Francis. She wants to pack up his belongings, meet his friends."

"She's your ex?" I asked.

"You've been doing your homework, huh?" John sighed. "Yeah, we were together for almost ten years."

"When did it end?"

"Just after I got this job. She was so happy for David, that I'd gotten him this amazing opportunity. He was a nurse but he really wanted to be an actor. He'd been in L.A. but wasn't getting much traction there. Then he came here, and things were going great for him, but they went south just as fast. Anyway, sorry. I should've told you this stuff earlier. I'm kind of out of my league here."

He rubbed his eyes, then took my empty cup and stacked it under his. He opened the window and aimed both cups at a nearby garbage can. To our collective shock, he made them in.

"Did you see that?!" he asked. "Holy crap, that's never happened in my entire life!"

As we drove back to the apartment complex, John told me more about growing up with David G. How he was the star of all the school plays. About David G's ex, Chloe, and how they were engaged when he broke it off. About the one time David G beat the high score at their bowling alley and offered to buy beers for everyone but only had $23 to his name. About how he always wanted to be famous, ever since he was a little kid. It was surreal learning about the normal, *before* life of a reality TV star. And a dead one at that.

John turned quiet after those few stories. We kept the AC on high and turned on a local radio station, just as the DJ started to play "Red Red Wine." John knew all the words and softly sang along.

We finally arrived back at the crew lot and pulled into a parking spot. John turned off the van. Neither of us moved to unbuckle our seatbelts. He turned to face me.

"Luella, there are people on this show who will do anything to succeed. They will lie, they will cheat, and they will ruin their own lives in the process."

"Who?" I asked.

John began wringing his hands. "You don't know what kind of environment you're dealing with here."

"It is weird here," I added.

He exhaled. "That night you found him... I admit I was acting a little crazy. I just didn't want it to be real. David G was like a little brother to me. I knew things were getting out of hand, but I didn't know how far until... Until he was lying there in your fucking bathtub."

He slammed the wheel then, and it honked. We both jumped.

"Sorry, ask me anything you want. I'm an open book," he said.

"What's with the key fobs?" I asked.

He sighed. "It was Striker's idea. Thought it would foster a community feel, something like that."

"Huh. And why'd you and Francis break up?"

"She didn't understand what it's like here. David was having sex with the wrong people, doing drugs, getting into fights. He was a mess, basically." John's voice became strained. "The guy was ruining his own life. Always exhausted and run down... that's not what a 21-year-old is supposed to act like. And she blamed me for everything! But what could I have done to stop it?"

That sparked something for me. "He was sick a lot?" I asked.

"Oh, all the time. He'd show up late to set with a million excuses. He was "hungover," he "must've had a bad batch of coke." I was angry at him. He was embarrassing me! I got him this job! I know he's dead, but I guess I'm still angry. He had everything going for him, and he ruined it."

John punched the steering wheel again then broke down in tears. We both sat there for a minute, John weeping and me looking at the dirty car floor.

"He didn't ruin it. Someone else did. This was a homocide," I said.

John blew his nose on a leftover Scoopy's napkin. "How do you know for sure?"

I put my hand on his shoulder. "A dead body can't put himself in a bathtub."

29

I checked the time — it was already 5:10 p.m. I was supposed to meet AJ in my apartment ten minutes ago. I thanked John for the ride and the milkshake and made a run for my apartment building. By the time I got to my door it was 5:14, and I was relieved not to find AJ waiting for me. Maybe he was running late, too. Maybe I'd beat him there? I wished I had his phone number.

I swiped my key fob, opened the door, and nearly screamed. There was AJ, sitting on my couch, eating handfuls of Cool Ranch Doritos from a family-sized bag. I thought back to the crumbs I'd found stuck to my face a couple days ago — maybe they weren't from a long-ago previous tenant. I couldn't think about that now.

"What are you doing?!" I yelled.

He wiggled his key fob in my general direction. "Breaking into your apartment — ha ha! What is *up*? Marie, how crazy is it that we're both here? Aren't you, like, forty?"

I glared at him. "I'm 29. Same age as your cousin. And it's *Luella*."

"I don't get it, what's with the *Luella*?" he said, sucking the Cool Ranch flavor off his fingers, one by one. "Want a chip?"

I shook my head. "It's an alias."

"Sick alias," he said sarcastically. "Wait, so why are you here?"

"I'm investigating."

"Oh yeah! My cousin was telling me about how you abandoned your whole life and now you're claiming to be some fancy private detective!" AJ laughed and grabbed another handful of chips. "So, who killed him?!"

"I'm trying to find out!"

"Shit, that's scary. You think the killer's someone in the cast? I bet it's Tasha."

I sat down in the chair adjacent to the couch. "Why Tasha?" I asked.

He shrugged. "Boobs of a murderer."

I rolled my eyes at him, and he laughed again, hard. He always had a great laugh, even as a kid. Boisterous and raspy, it was contagious. There wasn't a whole lot I missed from Staten Island, but I did miss hearing someone laugh like that.

"Just be careful," I told him.

He suddenly looked concerned. "Really?"

"I wouldn't trust anyone, AJ."

He stood up and paced. All his life, he could never really sit still.

"It's just, like, everyone I've met so far has been super nice. Tonight I'm supposed to meet up with a few of the guys from the cast. We're all going to the gym together."

"Sounds nice," I said. It all sounded a bit wholesome for the *Sex Island* crew, but I didn't think much of it at the time.

"Marie — sorry, Luella — um, if it's alright, I'm gonna do my thing here. I get you're here to solve a murder, and that sucks. But I'm here to have fun and meet girls and do my thing. They said I could win $100,000. That would, like, totally change my life, y'know?"

"Yeah."

"It's nice to see you and all, and I wanna be friends, but I really wanna do a good job on the show." He paused. "We cool?"

"Totally," I said. I felt a lump in my throat, but I wasn't sure why.

"Come here, give me a hug," he said. He held out his tattooed arms, and I stood up and hugged him.

"Hey, uh, sorry for trying to have sex with you before. For the record, I thought you were hotter with the brown frizz." He gave a little tug to my wig and laughed again. I found myself smiling and walked him to the door.

"The Marie stuff is our secret?" I asked.

"Scout's honor. I hope you find the son of a bitch." He paused, shuffling his feet. "Hey, um, what do you think of Blair?"

"She's hot and mean… everything you'd want in a reality show girlfriend. Why?"

He smiled. "Wish me luck."

"Good luck!" I said as I opened the door. He walked out and down the hall a few steps, then turned around.

"Hey, you should give my cousin a call sometime. She's miserable. Fuckin' hates Staten Island."

"Who doesn't?" I said.

He laughed, saluted me, and walked toward the elevator bank. The next day AJ wasn't on set.

30

THURSDAY

Isa walked me to set that Thursday morning, as usual. Her long, red hair was done up in a tight ballerina bun. She mentioned taking a double dose of Adderall an hour prior, and that she "felt amazing." She was moving at the speed of a rabbit in danger, which was 30 miles per hour according to that carrot magazine at the police station. In the middle of our walk, she turned to me, grabbed both my shoulders, and sang that entire *Pirates of Penzance* song, "I Am The Very Model of A Modern Major-General." Isa reminded me of a kid at a sleepover after too much Mountain Dew. By the time we arrived at the trailers, we both were in hysterics. This was all before I knew AJ was missing.

We were about to get to my trailer when I froze. Fifty feet away, I noticed a tall man with curls standing at the edge of the parking lot and staring at Isa and me. Even from far away, I could sense the anger in his body. His raised shoulders, his clenched fists. He looked an awful lot like that new guy, Justin, who'd been eliminated after one day on set.

"Isa," I said, nodding toward the strange man. "Isn't that Justin?"

She was still giggling. "What? Where?"

"Behind you, fifty feet," I said.

She abruptly turned, spotted him, then just as quickly, turned back to me. Subtlety wasn't Isa's thing.

"Oh shit, that is definitely Justin. He shouldn't be here. I'll go say something to him." She started walking purposefully toward him.

"No, Isa, don't!" I insisted. If it truly was Justin, I needed a bit more time to observe him.

"Oh fine!" she chirped. "But if he gets any closer, call me!"

With that, she ran off toward set. I looked back to where the man had been standing, but he was gone. Who needed coffee when one could start their morning like this.

I changed into my costume — today it was denim overalls and a bikini. I walked out of my trailer looking like a fifth-grader at a pool party, but I didn't hate it. AJ's trailer was three doors down from mine, so I headed over to say hi. I wanted to know how his night with the guys went. Also, I felt weird about how we left things, and I wanted to remind him that on set, I was *Luella*, not *Marie*.

I knocked on his door, but no one answered. After a minute, I let myself in. His trailer was empty, save for a pair of freshly pressed swim trunks hanging over a chair and a tray of snacks. Little wax-covered cheese rounds, apple sauces, those granola bars that were just nuts glued together... What the hell was going on here? I knew I wasn't a real contestant, but still, I never got any snacks! Inside his mini fridge were seltzers, Gatorades, name-brand energy drinks. Okay, this was sexism, plain and simple, but I was getting too distracted by the amenities. Where was AJ?

It seemed out of character for him not to show up on time during his first week on the job, especially after he told me how excited he was. There was a call sheet on his dressing table. I double-checked — his call time was the same as mine: 6 a.m. It was now almost 7. He must've overslept. I traced my finger across the call sheet and there was his phone number. I gave him a call, but it just rang and rang and rang. Very odd.

I know Luella's made some mistakes, and big ones at that. I was basically a rookie compared to most private eyes out there. But what I lacked in experience, I tried to make up for in listening skills and basic intuition. I don't know why, but I sensed at that moment that something terrible might've happened to AJ. That whatever or whoever had gotten to David G was on to their next victim, and I needed to move fast if I was going to stop AJ from meeting the same fate. I would not have Baby AJ's blood on my hands.

Phil's trailer was next to AJ's, and I figured he might know something about AJ's whereabouts. At the very least, he must've seen him with the guys at the gym hang. I ran up his trailer's noisy metal stairs and banged on the door.

"Phil!" I yelled. "Phil! Open up!"

Finally, Phil answered the door looking very concerned. "What's wrong, hon?" he asked.

"Have you seen AJ?" I tried to breathe and keep the fear out of my voice.

"Come in, come in, come in."

He put his arm around me and sat me down on the small vinyl couch. He took a seat in the recliner. Phil had a candle burning that made the place smell like vanilla. He took a couple of cold bottled waters from his mini fridge and tossed one to me.

"You okay?" he asked, a small crease forming between his perfectly symmetrical eyebrows.

"Have you seen AJ?" I opened the bottle and took a sip. It was so cold, I choked a little.

"Not since yesterday on set. Why?"

"What about the gym hang?"

"What are you talking about?" he asked.

It occurred to me then that maybe Phil wasn't invited to the guys' gym hang. Sarah had mentioned Phil mostly stayed to himself.

"Last night, AJ said…" I began, when Phil's face clouded over.

"You saw him last night?"

"We're old friends," I said.

He avoided eye contact, opting to look out the plastic window instead.

"Cool," he nodded to himself.

"So no gym?" I asked.

"I work out at home. You saw my place." He paused, as if to regather his thoughts. His voice became creakier.

"You know, I came on this show thinking it was going to be attractive people meeting each other, having a good time. I'm attractive, right? I can have a good time, right?" He was still looking out the window.

"Totally," I said, not sure what he was even asking me. I looked around and noticed the photograph of the woman on the vanity was no longer there.

"There are so many social dynamics at play, it's crazy," he continued. "You have to be cool and funny, and fit in with the guys. It's not fair. If it were just about meeting women and having sex on TV, I know I could win, but there's just so much bullshit." Phil chugged the rest of his water and crushed the plastic bottle in one fluid motion.

I felt bad for upsetting Phil, maybe I'd hit a raw nerve. But I had more pressing needs at the moment, namely, learning AJ's whereabouts.

"I'm sorry. I didn't mean…"

He finally made eye contact. "No, I'm sorry. Sometimes this show just gets to me."

I nodded. "I should find AJ," I said.

"Sure, sure. Go," he said. He stayed seated in his chair, so I let myself out. As I opened the door, I heard him blow out the candle. Another memorable interaction with Phil for the books.

31

I decided to try Nate's trailer next. Out of the three guys remaining — Nate, David N, and Ethan — I thought Nate might be the most willing to talk to me. He seemed friendlier than the other two, more approachable. Maybe it was because I'd seen him cry or maybe it was the whole "being Christian" thing. I knocked on Nate's trailer, but no one answered. I tried the knob but it was locked. David N's trailer was next door, so I tried his next.

As a viewer of the show, I always felt kinda bad for David N. It was the general consensus he was the lesser of the two Davids. Compared to David G, he was less attractive, less interesting, and he made a weird noise when he climaxed. He sounded like a horse saying hi to another horse. His claim to fame was that he'd never dumped anyone, that he'd always been the dump-ee, even in relationships prior to the show. Because of that, he was seen as a frequent and reliable rebound. He'd only started sleeping with Sarah after David G broke up with her.

"Who is it?" yelled a low voice from within.

"Luella," I said.

I heard two or maybe three voices discuss something I couldn't quite make out.

"One sec," the same low voice bellowed.

David N answered the door wearing a robe and pajama pants with dancing penguins on them. He stepped out and mostly closed the door behind him, accidentally leaving it open a small crack. I could sense movement behind the door.

"What's up?" he asked flatly.

"Busy?" I asked.

"Nope."

I squinted up at him. For some spiteful reason the sun had moved directly behind David N's narrow head, nearly blinding me to look at him.

"Seen AJ?" I asked.

"The new guy? No, sorry," he said, with his left hand already back on the door knob.

"Go to the gym last night?"

He shook his head. "Nah. Nate and Ethan came over and we watched a movie."

"What movie?" I asked.

He paused. "*Mighty Ducks.*" He paused again. "Actually *Mighty Ducks 2.*"

"Both?"

"No… yeah, uh… just *Mighty Ducks 2.*"

This guy was a worse liar than Stephanie and John combined. Everyone knew the sequel to *Mighty Ducks* was not called *Mighty Ducks 2*. It was called *D2: The Mighty Ducks*. He would've known that if he'd just watched the movie the night before.

"Is AJ with you?" I asked, nodding at his trailer door.

"No, I'm alone," he said. The way he stared at me, with his jaw slightly open, he looked like the world's skinniest caveman. He still hadn't shaved off that pathetic goatee.

"Luella, I gotta get ready. See ya."

He opened his trailer door just enough so he could slip back in without me seeing inside. I knew earlier I'd heard at least three voices. Who didn't want me to know they were in there?

So far, nobody had admitted to going to the gym with AJ. Had AJ lied to me? And was I supposed to believe that the night before, three 21-year-old guys sat quietly on a couch together watching the sequel to *The Mighty Ducks*, where the quack attack is back and they face off against Team Iceland in the Junior Olympics? David N was full of shit.

I wanted to know who else was in that trailer with David N. Maybe AJ was inside, and all this worry was for nothing. I looked at the time — it was 7:20 a.m. Everyone would have to come out of there eventually. I'd just have to employ the oldest trick in the private investigator's handbook: sitting and waiting. I looked around for a hideout spot and spotted the medic's trailer directly across the way. Jackpot.

The show's medic was a woman named Sheila. She was 55 years old with bleach-blonde hair, and she wore enough purple eye shadow for twelve additional eyes. Sheila was one of those new-age types who believed anything could be cured with a clove of garlic, including but not limited to athlete's foot and all cancers.

From the outside, I could see Sheila's trailer was equipped with a daybed that was pushed up against her front window. I assumed this was for the ill and infirmed. It would be a near perfect surveillance spot as long as I could stomach hearing about the virtues of raw garlic for an hour. I knocked on her door and told her I had a mysterious stomachache. She instructed me to lie down on the daybed right away while she made a fresh batch of "spicy broth for the tum-tum." I could not believe this woman had a medical license.

Here are a few of the direct quotes I heard Sheila say while I stared out the window waiting for anyone to leave David N's trailer:

"If fruit is nature's candy, then ginger is nature's sexy little girlfriend."

"I got the vaccine — it's called garlic!"

"The human body can actually process raw pork with ease."

"I start my day with two raw eggs and a whole loaf of bread, and just look at me. I'm a perfect human specimen!"

I was halfway done with my "spicy broth for the tum-tum" — an actually pleasant tasting chicken broth with a generous amount of turmeric and garlic in it — when I finally saw movement. David N's trailer door swung open and of all people, Stephanie walked out, followed by Nate. No AJ. Stephanie looked both ways then made her brisk, purposeful way toward set. Nate stalked off in the opposite direction.

Sheila caught me watching Stephanie from the window and cleared her throat.

"You know, I don't like to talk out of school, but that woman is so darn mean. I saw her screaming at David G that Friday before he disappeared. Yelling and screaming, and she didn't care who heard her. She was mad, mad, mad, mad, mad."

I turned toward Sheila. "Why?"

She popped a clove into a garlic press and squeezed. "Well, why do you think? He dumped her!"

So, maybe David N was Stephanie's latest rebound? But the question remained: what was Nate's involvement? And why were they all hiding from me? Regardless, I needed to find AJ, and hopefully still alive. My plan was thorough enough. I would sneak off set and search his apartment. If he wasn't in there, I'd search Nate's and David N's, then Stephanie's and George Striker's, Tasha's, then everyone's. I told Sheila I was all better and she nodded knowingly.

"Thank the magical tum-tum broth! It always worked on David G. He was in here all the time. Don't tell anyone, but I was rooting for him to win."

David G was in there all the time? I thought of Detective Johannes' story about the wife gradually poisoning the husband, but I didn't have time to think about that now. I ran out of Sheila's trailer and sprinted through several busy crew members as I made my way toward the apartment complex. I needed to work faster than I'd been working. Another life was on the line now. My heart was pounding. I was running fast, mostly looking behind to see if anyone was chasing after me. And that's when I collided head-on with Isa. We both fell backward, and I heard my own bones thud loudly against the pavement. Never a good thing.

"Damn, Luella, watch where you're going!" She examined her palms, which were scraped but not yet bleeding. I noticed a small tattoo on her inner wrist I'd never seen before. A solid black skull with cross bones underneath, like a poison symbol. I wouldn't have tagged Isa for a goth gal, but I had Betty Boop and her little dog on my lower back, so who's to judge what tattoos a person gets and why (for example, being 22 and drunk in Atlantic City).

I had landed hard on my ass, and I feared one of those tailbone injuries that can never be fixed. Sheila would be feeding me garlic for the rest of my days. I would become one of those people who brought an inflatable seat donut with them wherever they went. It'd have a smell people couldn't pinpoint, but they'd learn to associate it with me.

Isa got up first and dusted herself off, then helped me to my feet. She was wearing a whistle and dressed head to toe like a referee. Something weird was happening.

"C'mon, let's go to set!"

"I can't... I left something back at the apartment," I said.

"Sorry, Striker says all cast must report for today's shoot," she said.

"Have you seen AJ yet?" I asked her.

"Not yet, but he's probably already on set. Those new guys are always early. Now, don't make my job harder than it already is. Let's go!" She clapped her hand right on my tailbone, and I felt such severe pain, I shivered.

"Ow!" I screamed, but she'd already locked elbows with me and begun walking at a much faster pace than I was comfortable with. If Striker said all cast must report, hopefully AJ was already there. Hopefully there was nothing to worry about.

32

That Thursday, I can say with certainty, was one of the worst days of my life. And I have spent several days in Staten Island divorce court. I arrived at the beach hut to find nine little silk flags pushed into the sand. Waving in the sea breeze, they reminded me of elementary school field days. Their athletic connotation was unnerving.

Four of the flags were light pink and five were light blue. I had a feeling we were about to do some kind of horrible gender contest, and I was already dreading it. My tailbone alternated between throbbing and stabbing pain. Whenever I slightly tilted my head, I would hear my neck crack four times. Whatever we were about to do, I was not physically equipped. *Sheila, take me back,* I thought.

By the time I got there, Ethan, Nate, and Blair were already lined up a few feet in front of the flags. Shortly after me, David N, Sarah, and Tasha arrived. Phil was the last cast member to get to set. AJ, of course, never showed.

Isa blew her whistle and instructed each of us to grab a flag. The women were told to get pink, the men to get blue. One blue flag remained in the sand. My mind flashed to that bathtub, imagining AJ's face where David G's had been. I shook my head to get rid of the thought (my neck cracked four times). That kind of thinking was not productive. I had two objectives today and I needed to stay on track — figure out who was lying to me and find AJ before it was too late.

What the producers had planned for us that day turned out to be nothing short of a marathon. A marathon on steroids. We were to run around the beach trying to find as many flags as we could. There was only one rule: men could only pick up blue flags and women could only pick up pink ones. Some would be in plain sight, others would be more inconspicuous. The man and woman holding the most flags at the end of this straight-from-hell challenge would be granted immunity, which meant they'd be able to stay on the show for a couple extra days, even if they had terrible sex.

As you know, the cast of *Sex Island* originally started off with thirty people. Fifteen men, fifteen women. We were thirty-one episodes into the forty-episode season, which meant that the people who were still here had worked hard for it. If no more wild cards were added, each of the existing cast members had a fairly high chance of winning the grand prize of $100,000. Of course, they split it — a man and a woman were supposed to win together, so each would walk away with $50,000 and about a three-month window to become famous outside of the show. Last season's winners, Jessica D and Allen, weren't quite so fortunate. I heard Jessica D had been in and out of rehab. Allen went to jail for tax evasion. Show business sure had a way of chewing people up and spitting them out.

Isa blew her whistle again, this time for about ten seconds straight. The lung capacity on these youths! I thought maybe I could use this time to sidle up to Nate or Ethan, ask them if they'd heard from AJ. But the second the whistle blew, the cast scattered off in different directions, looking like water bugs when the light turned on. Cameramen were jogging with seventy pounds of equipment trying to keep up. Above us, several drone cameras captured the madness, too. The drones would make sneaking off to the apartment complex more challenging.

I found it painful to move with my tailbone the way it was, so I walked slowly. Blair ran past me and assumed my lackluster pace was some sort of strategy.

"If you think you can come in here as a wild card and actually win this thing, I'll kill you," she said, spittle forming on the sides of her mouth. She looked rabid.

Blair ran off, kicking sand in my face as she went. Maybe this show was more cutthroat than I had assumed. I wandered closer to the reeds, hoping it'd be a less confrontational destination. Sand had gotten in my mouth, and I felt the grit between my fake molars. I leaned over to spit, and that's when I saw it.

A little pink flag billowed in the wind. I felt a thrill I hadn't felt since my high school field hockey games. I parted the reeds with my hands and tiptoed through, careful to avoid any lingering crabs or whatever the hell else managed to live there. I snatched up the flag and beamed. Count 'em, Luella had two.

I walked with purpose now. Maybe slow and steady did win the race. I felt more alert and awake than I had in months. I visualized the next little pink flag — where would it be?

I'd taken off my heels, but the sand was getting hot. I walked toward the shore where it was cooler. With the sun shining above, the water looked a true cerulean blue. It was a color that made you think no human had ever peed in this part of the ocean. It felt good to walk there. The waves lapped softly at my ankles. The wet sand was pillowy beneath my feet.

I knew I should be finding AJ, finding David G's killer. That I shouldn't be wandering around a beach doing a stupid field day.

Honestly, what *was* I doing here? How had I let this undercover job veer so far in the wrong direction? I told myself once I got through this challenge, I'd be back on track, and I'd find AJ.

But then I saw another one. My third little pink flag. Floating there in the shallow water. I grabbed it, feeling for the first time in a while, a small, bright sense of victory. I had three flags! I was nearly a mile from set now, and I hadn't seen anyone for almost half an hour. The sun was getting hotter. The further I walked from set, the more debris I encountered. Old plastic bottles, broken shells, tampon dispensers, bottle caps. I wanted to make a George Striker apartment joke, but there was no one to tell it to, and besides, they would've had to have been inside his apartment to get it. I laughed out loud at my own logic. Now I knew I was getting overheated. I needed to get into the shade and drink some water.

I didn't know how long I'd been walking when I noticed a little wooded area. It was much cooler in the shade of the palm trees, and the sand was much rockier. There was still a dull, pulsing ache in and around my tailbone, but at least I'd gotten out of direct sunlight. I wanted to rest but wasn't sure how to sit down without causing severe pain. Maybe I could lie face down on the ground for a little while. All the crabs and beach spiders could make me their queen.

I was startled out of my daydreaming by a strong push from behind. One hand on my shoulder, one hand on my rib cage. I landed on my stomach, and the wind was knocked out of me. For what felt like a full minute I lay there, stunned. Was it possible I tripped? I had just been thinking of lying down like this, maybe this was what they called *manifesting?* I got up on my hands and knees then felt a kick to the back of my head. I collapsed again. My face smashed against the rocky terrain. My mouth tasted like blood.

I must've passed out from the kick. When I woke up again, the sun was much lower in the sky, and I found myself lying face up. My tongue was dry and my skin felt tight, almost crispy. My vision was blurry but I could make out a dark beard right above me. A face with dark eyes came into focus. Ethan.

My adrenaline kicked in, and I tried to scramble away on my elbows. My forehead hit his forehead, and he reeled backward, screaming. I needed to get away from him. I tried rolling over and standing, but my knees were too weak. I toppled to the ground, feeling around for a sharp stick or a rock or anything I could use to protect myself.

"Stop, Luella, it's me! It's Ethan! I'm not gonna hurt you!" he yelled.

I'd heard that last line too many times to believe it. I found a medium-sized stone and hurled it in his direction. It hit him in the neck, and he yelped in pain. I curled my fingers around a small, broken conch shell. Even if I couldn't get up, I would be ready for him.

"Please! Please, stop! Luella, I'm not trying to hurt you, I swear! You were out cold! Just listen to me! I don't want to hurt you!" he said slowly, carefully annunciating every word.

Ethan's neck was starting to bleed where the rock hit him. He held up both hands and looked at me with pleading eyes. I stared at him. Was it possible he *was* just here to help me? He extended his hand, and I grabbed it hesitantly, wincing as my body registered its injuries. I couldn't properly stand and found myself leaning against his strong frame to steady myself. He was warm to the touch and drenched in sweat. I could smell his natural musk, which was not altogether unpleasant. I looked up at the sun. I must've been out for hours. I didn't want to think about the state of my stupid wig.

"Come on, let's take you back," he said, in a gentler voice than I'd ever heard him use.

After too many failed attempts, we both concluded that me walking was out of the question. For most of the journey back, he ended up carrying me like a damn baby. Together we must've looked like the saddest and dirtiest 1950s newlyweds.

Eventually, we made it back to the apartment complex. He asked which room I was staying in, and I told him, "4E." He used his key fob to get in, then gently set me down on the couch. He brought me a glass of cold water and dabbed my forehead with a washcloth he'd wrapped around ice cubes. We didn't speak much. In the back of my mind, I knew he would probably see my wigs but I couldn't summon the energy to hide them. I was disappointed in myself. By that time, I had a strong feeling AJ was already dead.

When I think back to that night — the night I saw Ethan's odd nurturing side — one thing stuck out. The entire time he was cleaning my wounds, cooling my forehead with washcloths, bringing a water glass to my lips, he never once looked at me.

33

The sun had set, and I still hadn't moved from the couch. I had been drifting in and out of consciousness, but now I was awake. The light in the kitchenette was on, but nothing else. My face felt swollen, and I could tell my Luella teeth were askew. I ran my tongue over them and tasted dry blood. I thought maybe Ethan had left, but after I started to stir, he came out of my bedroom and took a seat on the leg of the couch.

"Hey," I said.

"Hey sleepyhead. It's getting to be dinner time. You want something? I was gonna order Thai food."

"I'm good," I said.

"I'll get you a soup," he said, already in the midst of calling the restaurant. "Hi. Yeah, same address as usual. Can I get a chicken pad Thai, a chicken green curry, and a pineapple fried rice?" He paused while the person on the other end asked a question. "Uh, let's go with chicken. And a tom yum soup. Thanks." He hung up and stood, clasping his hands behind his back.

"Dinner will be served in forty-five minutes to an hour," he said, speaking like an old British butler. Was he really joking around with me? This was a side of Ethan I had never seen.

"Your George Striker impression?" I asked. My words came out muffled. Some part of my teeth was definitely broken.

Ethan's face fell. "He's not so bad."

At the mere idea of someone defending Striker, I felt my chest tighten in rage. At least the anger was a nice distraction from the pain.

"He tried to drug me," I said, sounding like I had about eighteen cotton balls in my mouth.

He let out a small laugh of disbelief. "There's no way. George wouldn't do that. He's..." he trailed off. "Just trust me."

I tried to sit up. "What's with you two?"

Ethan's face reddened. "Me and George Striker? Nothing. We're friends."

"Is he helping you?" I asked.

"I mean, sure... friends help each other," he said, shrugging.

"You think you'll win?" I asked.

"I certainly hope so. This show is humiliating. You think I wanna do all this bullshit to walk away with nothing? No way. You know how much I'm getting paid to be here?"

I knew the starting contract was low. But I figured that someone like Ethan, who'd made news headlines and become one of the show's stars, might earn something more.

He continued, "Three hundred dollars a week. I made more working at a gas station in Podunk freaking Kansas. If I don't win, this whole thing's been a complete waste of time."

"Then I hope you win," I said.

He shrugged. "I mean, I think I stand a chance! Especially now that David G's gone."

I looked at him skeptically.

"I just meant that he was the frontrunner," he stammered. "And everybody knew it. It sucks that he's gone, though. It's all really sad."

With the heat and the attack, I'd temporarily forgotten what I was there to do, and most importantly, that time was of the essence. I began to panic, and mustered all my energy to peel myself off the couch.

"What's wrong?" he asked.

"Last night — were you with AJ?" I asked, searching his eyes.

"No?" Ethan looked confused. "Hey, where was he today? I didn't see him on set."

I tried to stand up, but my body was slow-moving. I felt a surge of pain shoot from my tailbone to my neck.

Ethan stood in front of me. "Now, where do you think you're going?" he asked, his tone verging on aggressive. I shot him a look, and he backed down quickly.

"I just meant the food's coming, and you're hurt, so... I wasn't trying to..."

"How was *Mighty Ducks 2*?" I asked.

"What?"

Someone knocked then. We both turned toward the door.

"Must be dinner. I'll get it," he said.

Ethan opened the door, and a charged silence ensued. I gathered that whoever was at the door was not there to deliver our dinner.

"What the hell are *you* doing here?" Ethan's tone was angry, but from where I was situated on the couch, I couldn't see who the other person was.

"Same question, bro," I heard a man's voice say. A familiar voice. Phil.

Phil strutted past Ethan into the living room, holding a Tupperware of what looked like red Jell-O. He knelt down in front of the couch so we were nearly face to face.

"Oh baby, look at you. What happened?" Phil asked, gently stroking my wig.

Ethan walked up behind him, his arms crossed in front of his chest.

"She was attacked during the challenge. I found her on the ground."

Even with Ethan looming over him, Phil didn't take his eyes off me. "That's so scary. Are you okay?" Phil kept petting my wig. I tried to subtly brush his hand away.

"I'll be fine," I said, suddenly aware I probably looked as bad as I felt.

"Ethan, I can take over if you need a break. Looks like you've been on nurse duty for a while now." Only then did Phil look up at Ethan.

"Well, we've got food coming soon," Ethan said.

There was a palpable tension in the room. My eyes darted back and forth between the two men. Ethan glared at Phil, while Phil stared at me.

"I brought you Jell-O," Phil said. He jiggled the Tupperware and its contents danced malevolently. I have always hated Jell-O. My great-aunt Ruthie used to serve it for dessert. Like the woman had never heard of cake.

"Thanks," I said. "Maybe later."

Phil stood up, patting me on the head. "I'll just put it in the fridge for now."

He made his way to the kitchenette. Phil appeared to be quite at home here.

"I was worried — you both left before we wrapped today. You didn't even get to see how the challenge ended!" Phil said, scanning my mostly empty fridge.

"What happened?" Ethan asked with a forced nonchalance. I realized then that Ethan might have lost his chance at immunity by helping me.

"It was crazy! In the last hour, Tasha had, like, twelve flags, and Blair had ten. Then at the last minute, Blair tackled Tasha to the ground and managed to wrestle seven away. Blair got the immunity!"

Was it possible Blair had attacked me? Would my measly three flags be worth all that? I wondered where those flags were now.

"Who won the men's immunity?" Ethan asked, barely concealing his contempt.

Phil bowed his head. "You're looking at him. Guys, I just kept finding flags! I felt like I was really in my element today, you know? Felt good. Your boy found twenty-five flags, if you can believe it."

"Seems like you're the new frontrunner," Ethan said.

"New? Bro, I've *been* the frontrunner!" Phil said, making a *suck it* gesture with both hands.

"Yeah, right," Ethan muttered.

"What'd you say to me?" Phil said, pushing Ethan's shoulder.

"You want to fight, bro?" Ethan said, puffing out his chest. This was escalating awfully quickly.

"Nah, bro, not tonight. I'm feeling too good tonight. But I'll get you when you least expect it," Phil replied, winking at Ethan.

Ethan shook his head, then looked at his phone. "Well, congrats, man. Damn, it's late. I'm gonna get goin'."

"What about the food?" I asked.

"You guys eat it. I'm not hungry," Ethan said.

Ten seconds later, Ethan was out the door.

It was a bizarre interaction, but Phil didn't seem to register any of it. He made himself comfortable on the couch, scooting my legs over to make room for himself.

"Can I tell you where I found all the flags? It felt so intuitive out there. First one I found buried mostly in the sand, just the top of it was visible, but I've always had eagle eyes..."

For the next hour, Phil talked me through his twenty-five-flag conquest without coming up for air. He was on cloud nine. He talked about where he found them, how he found them, how his stamina was unbeatable, how strong he was. The Thai food arrived sometime in the middle of his monologue. He received the food, smelled it, then actually threw it in the garbage can.

"Trust me, that stuff is not good for you, babe. How about some Jell-O?"

If I had the energy, I would've thrown *him* in the garbage can.

Phil continued monologuing for another hour. He paced the apartment as he spoke. At one point I pretended to fall asleep, but he just kept on talking. At one point I thought I saw him walk in and out of my bedroom, but I was too exhausted to ask why. When he finally got the hint to go, he knelt down until his face was an inch away from mine.

"Don't forget to eat your Jell-O, babe," he whispered. I could smell the peppermint on his breath.

When I first met Phil, I thought he was hot but not so bright. The more I got to know him, I realized he was also completely obnoxious. That's when I knew he was going to win *Sex Island*.

34

FRIDAY

I woke up Friday morning and texted John first thing:

Any word from AJ?

John said he hadn't heard from him. What kind of show allowed people to go missing, and nobody did anything about it? It was either an issue of incompetence or collusion, and I wasn't sure which. I told John to contact the police and AJ's immediate family A.S.A.P. He said he would get on it. After nearly two weeks, I was starting to understand that show business only really responded to a squeaky wheel.

I told John somebody attacked me during the challenge, and that it could have been whoever went after David G and possibly AJ. He responded that if I needed to *take the day off and focus on self-care,* I could do that. Self-care! What a novel idea.

Was the attack captured on camera? I asked.

John said no. Turned out the cameras mostly followed Blair, Nate, and Sarah for the majority of yesterday's challenge. So, Blair might not have been my attacker after all. I thought of Justin, the new guy who'd been staring angrily at Isa and me at the beginning of the day. I wondered if he had something to do with this.

I managed to take a shower (look at me and my self-care!), and that's when I learned that my shoulders were severely sunburnt in the unfortunate shape of my overall straps. Everything hurt. I did a quick inventory of my aches and pains: head, spine, hips, tailbone, left foot, shoulders, and face. As I was drying off, I found a large green bruise on the back of my leg I didn't remember getting. I glanced in the fogged-up mirror. My face had little cuts all along the left side and my left cheek was bruised a yellowish-green color. My left eye was nearly swollen shut. All in all, stunning. Camera-ready. No notes.

The pigtail wig was in bad shape, so I resorted to backup wig number two. This one was significantly itchier than the others, but it looked a whole lot better than backup number three. It hurt my eye to put makeup on, so I opted for sunglasses. I went to put my teeth in and almost screamed. My Luella teeth were missing a tooth, and a front one, no less. My mind raced... how could I fix this, and fast?

Like I've said, a missing front tooth is like a car accident. No one can look away. It's the reason I started wearing the fake teeth in the first place. Part of why Luella works is that she has none of my visible flaws. She's sexy, she's demure, and she's definitely not missing a damn front tooth! I groaned and smacked my own forehead on repeat until it was numb. Why did this job feel so much harder than every other job I'd ever done?

Maybe that wasn't necessarily true, but I remember very little from the Taylor Bell case. That's why I started writing things down this time around.

There were days I couldn't believe I'd once been a functioning social worker, with clients and an office and everything. In some ways, I think doing that job enabled me to deal with my own shit so haphazardly, like a carpenter who lets her own house be destroyed by termites. Maybe if I'd done something else with my life, I wouldn't be doing this double-identity stuff now. Maybe I'd even be well-adjusted or something. Wouldn't that be nice.

I was losing it and needed to eat something. My to-do list was growing: find AJ, find David G's killer, fix my front tooth, find food. I debated eating the food Phil had thrown in the garbage last night, but I figured I should probably be kinder to my ailing body. I even considered Phil's Jell-O for half a second before the memories of Great Aunt Ruthie's Jell-O molds returned to haunt me. Her recipe called for Jell-O mix, mayonnaise, and peeled grapes. Good God.

I made my way down to the group pantry and got myself three bananas, a yogurt parfait, and a to-go cup of coffee the size of my femur. Standing there with the broken Luella teeth in my pocket, I ate the three bananas one right after the other, like a human Donkey Kong. I inhaled the parfait. I drank the coffee in big, burning gulps. Maybe after this gig, I'd have enough money to permanently replace my teeth with some nice-looking veneers. Dr. Frank would be down to do it, especially after he saw what I'd done to this pair.

I was zoning out and drinking the last sip of my coffee when I realized what could be the miracle solution to my tooth problem. I'd been unknowingly staring at it for the last five minutes. There in front of me was a jar of loose, white Chiclet gum. The go-to fake front teeth for generations of children the world over.

I took a handful up to my room and tried one on with my Luella teeth. It was soft and painfully minty, and I swore I felt the sugar slowly eroding my real tooth underneath, but it didn't look half bad. I should probably note, it also didn't look half good, but it would do the trick. Especially if I kept the talking to an absolute minimum.

My plan was to search the entire apartment building for AJ while the cast and crew were on set that day. I ransacked my apartment for John's list of where everyone lived. Finally I found it laying inside my notebook where I'd written the list of suspects. I hadn't remembered putting it there, but I didn't give it much thought at the time. I read the directory again, trying my best to memorize it:

~~David G - 7A~~
Ethan - ~~7E~~ 8A
David N - 7B
Phil - 7G
Nate - 7C
Blair - 7D
Tasha - 7H
Sarah - 4D
George - PH
Stephanie - 7F
John - 2A
Isa- 8D
Luella - ~~7E~~ 4E

I realized AJ's apartment wasn't listed, that this directory had been made before AJ joined the cast. I called his phone again, but it went straight to voicemail. I figured as much. I swallowed two extra strength Tylenol and headed out. My first stop would have to be Stephanie's place. Her behavior made me think she had something to hide.

35

Knowing she'd be at work, I scanned my key fob at Stephanie's door and got in, no problem. I was starting to think this George Striker community effort was the greatest thing to happen to the private detective industry in years.

Immediately, her apartment seemed different than it had before. The tapestry on the wall was gone, many of the homey touches now missing. The framed photos with family, the blanket, the tea kettle, all gone. Maybe she was in the process of decluttering... or had she really been putting on an act for me?

I stood in the entryway listening for any sounds of a trapped adult man within the apartment. Hearing nothing, I proceeded with caution, starting with the bedroom. The only thing under her bed was a ten-pound dumbbell covered in a thin layer of dust. I looked inside her closet, but all I found were heels, pencil skirts, and a couple blazers still in their plastic dry-cleaning bags.

I went through her drawers — not that I thought I would find AJ in her drawers — but maybe there'd be a clue or two. Everything was organized: orderly stacks of thong underwear, folded socks, three identical tan underwire bras, a four-inch paring knife. Okay, a four-inch paring knife was *interesting*. I wondered why someone would keep a knife in their underwear drawer. Perhaps as a warning to snooping people like me? I thought of the strange incision around David G's bellybutton. Could that have been done with a four-inch paring knife?

I moved on to the bedside table. People usually kept their personal goodies stashed away in these drawers. Inside I found a bottle of extra-strength melatonin, a car key, and a pile of six sticky notes. I pocketed the car key and read through the notes. It seemed Stephanie had something of a romance going on. In order, they said:

Call me 2nite

Bb gimme wut I need

Miss ur mouth, bb

Miss u bb :(

I luv u! I luv u! I luv u!

Luv you Stefie bb

Well, whoever this mystery author was, they were somewhat of a medium speller. Their handwriting was legible but their words tended to be written close together, the spacing uneven. I noticed that all the letters slightly slanted to the right. I'd read somewhere that if your letters slanted to the left, that meant you were introverted, but if they slanted to the right, that meant you craved human interaction. I tried to remember where I'd read that — most likely on the bottom of a Snapple cap. I gave the theory little weight.

The writer had employed various ball-point and gel pens but always wrote on yellow Post-it Notes. I could see the faint imprint of the words *Miss u bb :(* on the note that said *I luv u! I luv u! I luv u!* The notes must've been written on the same pad. It seemed what had started as a mostly sexual relationship between Stephanie and the writer had evolved over time into something more emotional, at least from the author's perspective.

I examined the top one again — the one that said *Call me 2nite*. I held the little yellow note up to the sun shining through Stephanie's bedroom window. I wanted to see if perhaps there was an imprint on this one, too — something to indicate who the writer was, other notes they'd written before this love tirade. I tilted the note and finally, the sun hit it just right. I saw what looked to be the faint imprint of some sort of list. I could only make out a few of the letters:

T__thpa__

Mout____

Milk

__gs

A list, a list… I thought about why people made lists. Possibly, it was a to-do list. Or a grocery list. *Milk* was a grocery. *Milk*, and then whatever *t…thpa…* was. Perhaps toothpaste? So, it was a grocery list! Milk, toothpaste, mouthwash. And eggs! Certainly not the most revealing grocery list of all time. If anything, it seemed almost *too* basic. I took a photo to study later on. I had several more apartments to get to before the end of the shoot that day.

The fact that Stephanie kept these notes in her bedside drawer did not escape me. She must've been emotionally invested. But why only six of them, I wondered. Maybe it was a short-lived romance.

I knew I should move on to the other apartments, but quickly, I wanted to check out her bathroom while I was there. On the sink, I found a bottle of Stella by Stella McCartney. I remembered loving that scent — the notes of amber and citrus. It had been discontinued years ago. How did she get her hands on a new bottle? The scent triggered something for me. That morning in my apartment when my teeth first went missing… this must've been the perfume I smelled.

I removed the cap and sprayed some on my wrist to be sure, which I only realized was a huge mistake right as I did it. I could picture the ensuing conversation going as such:

> Stephanie: *Hi Luella! Say, why do you smell like my discontinued eau de toilette, Stella by Stella McCartney?*

> Luella: *Well, Stephanie, it's a tale as old as time... I was in your apartment... looking for a missing man... and oh, did you know you have a knife in your underwear drawer? That's kinda weird!*

Sometimes I am very stupid. Like rocks-for-brain level stupid. I tried washing off the perfume and was in the midst of scrubbing away at my wrist when I heard a noise. Someone else was entering the apartment. I willed my body to move quickly and quietly into the shower, leaving a small gap between the plastic curtain and the wall so I might see who'd come in.

I heard whoever it was — *Intruder #2* — rummaging around in the kitchenette, then moving on to the living room. Based on the drawer slams and heavy breathing, it sounded like they were desperately looking for a specific something or someone, and they hadn't found it yet.

Whoever it was stormed into the bedroom. From where I was standing, I couldn't see much without being seen myself. I heard grunts, then some kind of bone-hitting-metal sound, and a man's voice letting out a strained "Mother-fuck!" It took a second but I soon registered the voice. What the hell was John doing here?

"John?" I called out from inside the shower curtain. Silence ensued.

"Luella?!" John called back, more confused than anything else. He limped into the bathroom and pulled back the shower curtain. We both looked at each other with a mix of shock and confusion.

"What are you looking for?" I asked him.

"I have the same question!" he replied. "And what the hell happened to your tooth?"

Dammit.

35A

Before we continue any further, I should say that intuition can be misleading. Whatever theories I had at that moment were just that: theories. I still had nothing in terms of cold, hard evidence.

I was being cautious this time. I didn't want to jump to conclusions. That was how I'd messed up the Bell case. I trusted my intuition and it blinded me to evidence that was staring me right in the face. I sent the wrong man to jail, and for that I will always feel responsible.

See, Julia Bell's murder was my biggest case yet. News outlets couldn't get enough of this beautiful missing woman. The police assumed her husband, Taylor Bell, did it. But Taylor was my client. I *knew* Taylor. He struggled with minor depression, some social anxiety. There was no way he killed his own wife.

It took three weeks to find her body. In the first week of her disappearance, Bell uncovered a series of sexy text messages between Julia and his best friend, Mark Lassiter. During a session, Taylor confessed to me he felt utterly shocked, betrayed, and alone. Like a dope, I believed him. Luella did some digging and found out Julia actually had been having an affair with Lassiter for the last six months prior to her disappearance.

This guy, Mark Lassiter, was a shady character, to say the least. He had prior arrests for domestic assault, and he didn't exactly "pay" his taxes. He was your run of the mill piece of shit. I found bloody gloves in the trunk of Lassiter's car, and the blood came back a confirmed DNA match to Julia Bell. I was convinced Mark Lassiter was the murderer.

My intuition told me to trust Taylor Bell, that he was telling me the truth. As his social worker, I never stopped to think that he'd fastidiously studied depression and anxiety prior to seeing me. That he'd pretended to have the symptoms of both, so when he finally did kill his wife (something he'd been premeditating for years), his social worker could testify that he would never, ever do such a thing. Poor, depressed Taylor Bell? No way!

Mark Lassiter was eventually released from jail after someone finally confirmed his alibi. He really had been at a Wagner Seahawks basketball game at the time of the murder. I tried to keep tabs on him for a while after that — Google alerts, questionably legal geotags, etc. — but he managed to move out of Staten Island and off the grid. I wondered where he was these days, what he was up to. Hopefully, he wasn't a fan of the nationally broadcast show, *Sex Island.*

This is all just to say why I was hesitant to jump to any conclusions, particularly about John Murphy.

36

Back to Stephanie's apartment, in which John and I were both independently breaking and entering. Since I was the private investigator and part of my job was rifling through other people's things, I insisted John explain himself first.

He hemmed and hawed for a while before getting to the point.

"I just... I'm trying to find something of hers, okay?" He seemed more flustered than usual.

"What?" I asked, still standing in the shower.

John closed the lid of the toilet, sat down, and put his head in his hands. He let out a long sigh, then looked up to the ceiling.

"I think Stephanie is hiding something. Something that could lead us to AJ. And help us figure out what happened to David G. That's why I'm here, okay?"

"You talk to AJ's family?" It was proving very difficult to talk with the Chiclet tooth. It was getting softer by the second.

He nodded. "I did. I told them we were doing everything we could to find him."

"What's with Ste... Stepa..." It turned out I could no longer pronounce *Stephanie* with the gum for a tooth. "What's with her?" I managed.

"There were rumors she was having an affair with David G just before he died. I mean, she was his boss," he said. "But what was I supposed to do about it? Say something to her?! This was my first year on the job. Anyway, if you want to know my theory, I think Stephanie killed David G because he threatened to tell the network. Then she got a taste for blood. Then she killed AJ."

My mouth went dry. "AJ's dead?"

"In this scenario, AJ is dead." He paused, then added, "which is very sad."

"Uh huh." My adrenaline was wearing off. The shooting pains in my tailbone had started up again.

"Luella, things have gone too far. So, I decided I'm going to help you solve this case. I'm not trying to mansplain or whatever. I just have a hunch, and I'm going for it. It's worth noting that this kind of go-get-'em attitude is what got me so far in TV production in the first place."

John was wearing thin on me. "Does Ste... does *she* own a car?" I asked.

"No, definitely not. Why? You need a car? I could get the passenger van again if you need a ride. That was nice, getting milkshakes with you."

"John, where does AJ live?" I asked.

"Um, I think we put him in 4A or 4B, maybe 4G? I'll have to double check," he said.

"Find out," I said, as I slowly climbed out of the shower and made my way to the front door. My legs were shaking and my back had begun to spasm. I felt like I had twenty minutes left before my body gave out again.

"Wait, where are you going now?" John asked, following me like a 38-year-old Labrador Retriever.

I tried to think. AJ was new here. Where could he be? He disappeared sometime between the hours of 5:20 p.m. Wednesday and 6:00 a.m. Thursday. Maybe he was in one of the guys' places. It'd definitely be worth checking out. Or Blair! When he brought up Blair that evening, he'd said, "Wish me luck!" Maybe he was going to see Blair after he saw me!

"Blair's place," I replied, walking out the door. My pronunciation was so garbled, I must've sounded like I was drunk.

"Okay, I'm coming with you!" he said, closing a drawer he'd left open in the kitchenette. He shut Stephanie's door behind us.

We keyed into Blair's place, which on first impression, looked like a Lisa Frank acid nightmare. She'd painted the walls a neon violet color, which managed to give the already small apartment a claustrophobic quality. The place smelled like a peach vape. John started sneezing. Everywhere I looked I saw unicorns, kittens, and rainbows. If this was the inside of Blair's head, I was even more afraid of her than I thought.

Most notably, though, was Blair's choice of wall art. Hung everywhere were large framed nudes of Blair on horseback. There was Blair nude on a horse above the couch. And there was Blair nude on a horse in the kitchenette. And there was Blair nude on a horse holding a baseball bat (?!) next to the TV. Apparently Blair loved horses. I'd say she loved them too much.

John wasn't as thrown by the decor as I was. Maybe he'd been in there before. For a first-timer, it was too much to take in at once. This place was like the Metropolitan Museum of Rainbows and Horse Nudes. We walked into the bedroom, which more or less shared the same motif as the rest of the apartment — rainbows, sequins, a framed Blair naked on a horse.

John nudged me. "What are we looking for here?"

"Don't know," I said, scanning the room for something that might be out of place.

Then I saw the hat. The flat-brimmed Jets hat that AJ wore on his first day was sitting on Blair's dresser. My arms broke out in goosebumps. I tried to think — was he wearing the hat at my apartment Wednesday evening? I couldn't remember. I'd have to check the fourth floor security cameras. If AJ *was* wearing the hat, then Blair must've been who he went to see next. Maybe she was the last person he ever saw.

I tapped John on the shoulder. "The hallway security footage…" I mumbled.

"You wanna watch it? Which floor? Seven's been broken for at least a month now."

"Fourth floor," I tried to say. I gave up and resorted to holding up four fingers.

"No prob. I'll text the super now." He sneezed three times in a row. "We're like a detective duo, huh? Sherlock and Watson, baby! I should get me a pipe!"

John wandered back into the living room, fully engrossed in his phone.

I looked again at AJ's hat on Blair's dresser. I hoped it wasn't there as a hunting trophy.

John rushed back into the bedroom. "Shit. Francis's flight got in early. I should go pick her up from the airport. You good?"

"All good," I said, flashing him a peace sign. Honestly, I was relieved to get rid of him.

John dashed out. My strength was fading. I searched the apartment once more, but besides the hat and the poor horses, I found nothing too out of the ordinary. I decided Phil's place was next. I made sure Blair's door was shut and ambled over to Phil's across the hall. I waved my key fob and tried the door handle, but it didn't work. Usually a green light appeared, then the door would click open. Instead, the light was red. I tried again. Still red, and no click. Strange.

I felt my phone buzz in my pocket and checked it. Sophie had sent me a cute photo of Meatloaf curled up in a circle on the couch along with two text messages:

Your cat is in my spot

can I push it off couch?

I felt a pang of homesickness. I wondered how much longer I'd be on this island, how much longer until I had some answers. That reminded me to text Lauren.

Hey I'm sorry about AJ. I'm gonna find him, ok?

Three dots appeared, then disappeared. Lauren was calling me. I picked up.

"Hey," I said.

"What the hell is going on with my cousin?" I could hear Lauren's breathing. She was running.

"Didn't John talk to your family?" I asked, hoping there'd been a mistake, hoping she could understand me through the broken teeth.

"Who is John? No one's said anything to us. But AJ wasn't on the show yesterday. What is going on, Marie?!"

I took a deep breath and filled her in on everything I knew so far. At least my intuition was correct on one thing — John could not be trusted.

37

I told Lauren I'd keep her in the know from here on out. I didn't want to believe John was purposely lying to me — I felt like I'd let him in that morning, and I already regretted it. My head was spinning. I needed to go back to my room, drink some water, take a nap, eat something. By that point, I think I'd swallowed the gum tooth because it was no longer in the front of my mouth.

I was walking toward the elevator bank on the seventh floor when I heard what sounded like air escaping from a tire. I stopped and waited for the noise to repeat. A few seconds later, I heard it again. The sound was coming from the trash room across the elevators. I tried my key fob, and the door opened. Immediately I was confronted with a strong animal odor.

Inside the trash room, I saw what looked like a human leg behind three large trash bags. My breath caught in my chest. I shoved the bags out of the way, and underneath, I found AJ lying on the ground unconscious. His wrists were tied together and so were his ankles. His mouth had been duct-taped shut. A trail of dried blood looked like it came from his nose. I felt a faint pulse and immediately called 911. I asked for an ambulance and the police.

I knelt down and whispered to him, "It's going to be okay," as I gently pried the duct tape off his mouth. If it hurt him, he didn't show it. His eyelids barely fluttered. I repeated over and over, "AJ, I'm here. AJ, it's going to be okay."

The minutes went by like hours. The ambulance arrived first, then the police. Detective Johannes got there and gave me a nod. Stephanie must have heard the sirens from set. She followed the police into the apartment building, insisting that she was an executive producer and that she be told what was going on. I could hear her yelling from the elevators. When the doors opened, she came face to face with AJ's limp body on a stretcher. She was finally speechless.

She looked at me. "What happened to him?" Her voice was shaky. I told her how I'd found him. She cleared her throat and excused herself to make some calls. I didn't know quite what to make of her.

The police busied themselves dusting for fingerprints and photographing the crime scene, so I excused myself to call Lauren again. I let her know what happened, and she sounded grateful for the update. Two friends reuniting over an almost-dead cousin. It sounded like its own horrible Lifetime movie.

I went back to my place to lie down. I looked at the time — somehow it wasn't even noon. I took another dose of Tylenol and curled up on the couch. The next thing I knew, I woke up to someone knocking on my door. I felt groggy and stiff and like someone had hit me with a car. I'd unfortunately napped with the wig on. My scalp was so itchy I thought my brain was going to explode.

I answered the door. John stood there with a petite woman in her late twenties I took to be Francis, David G's sister. She had dark, shoulder-length hair and David G's same eyes. Francis introduced herself and shook my hand. I smiled and saw them both register my missing front tooth at the same time. I quickly pulled my shirt over my mouth and kept it there. Turtle mode was the only solution.

"I was telling Francis on the ride over here how we're working together to solve the case," John said.

Was that why he decided to help me? To impress his ex-girlfriend?

"Can we come in?" he asked.

I rubbed my eyes. "Sure."

I led them into the living room, and they each took a seat on the couch. Sitting next to each other like that, they really did look like a couple. I went to my fridge to see what I could offer them in the world of refreshments. All I had was coffee and that Tupperware of Phil's red Jell-O.

"Jell-O? Coffee?" I asked.

Francis said yes to the coffee. John said yes to the Jell-O.

I put a pot on, scooped some Jell-O into a bowl for John, and joined them in the living room.

"I heard you found AJ!" John said, then turned to Francis. "It's the strangest thing — Luella keeps being the one to find these guys. She was the one to find your brother, too."

I wasn't sure I liked what John was implying. Francis spoke again, attempting to break the tension.

"I know you're doing a lot for my brother's case. If there's anything I can do to help, please let me know."

I nodded, the lower half of my face still inside the shirt.

"What was he like?" I asked.

"He was just…" Francis wiped a tear from her eye. "He was just so kind. He was a nurse, you know, and he wanted to be an actor, too. Like Patch Adams."

I didn't think that was like Patch Adams at all, but this was neither the time nor the place to correct her. She pulled out a tissue and blew her nose. Meanwhile, John ate his Jell-O like it had done something to his mother.

Francis continued, "He was a good guy. Always very trusting of people. Women adored him." She blew her nose again. "Excuse me, do you have a bathroom?"

I nodded and pointed her in the right direction. As she left the room, John followed her with his eyes. Once she was out of sight, he turned back to me, set down his empty dish, and pulled out his phone.

"So, the super sent video footage from the fourth floor hallway cameras. Look at this."

On his phone, I watched a grainy black and white AJ leave my apartment at 5:21 p.m., wearing his flat-brimmed Jets hat. It was very possible Blair was the last person he saw. Unless there was someone else after Blair.

"Wait, I gotta show you this other crazy thing," John said. He fiddled with his phone and then turned it toward me again.

"Security also sent me footage from the penthouse hallway. Look at this."

I watched as a grainy black-and-white Marie entered and eventually exited George Striker's apartment. My neck and scalp felt hot. John played the footage again, this time at half-speed.

"Like, who the hell is *that*?" he asked.

He paused the video where my face was most visible, then zoomed in closer using his thumb and forefinger. He looked back at me then, a smirk beginning to form in the corner of his mouth.

"Luella, I'd say *that's* our suspect, whoever that is."

38

John and Francis left my apartment soon after. Francis claimed she was tired from traveling, and John said he had to get back to set. Something had definitely shifted between me and John since that morning. Did he honestly think I was the one who killed David G and stored AJ in a trash room? The lady doth protest too much. He was starting to seem more and more like Stephanie.

I made my way back to the seventh floor trash room to see if there was anything I missed in the chaos of finding AJ. When I got there, the place was covered in police tape, but no one stood guard, so I snuck back in. The three trash bags that had been covering AJ's body had been pushed to the side by the paramedics, and the police hadn't touched them. They were still there. I figured whoever put AJ in there likely put those trash bags in there, too. I untied the largest one.

I looked inside and froze. The bag contained what must have been six empty gallon jugs. I picked one up and looked at the label. Prestone Antifreeze. Whoever's trash this was either had a ton of cars or a ton of people to slowly poison. I had a feeling whatever the killer had done to David G, he or she had also done to AJ.

The other two bags were filled with bedding. Sheets, pillows, and a black-and-white patterned comforter. I recognized them from every apartment I'd seen in that building. These were standard issue.

I wondered why someone would throw away a whole set of bedding. When I finally smelled it, I nearly keeled over. Vomit. Old vomit. I carefully sifted through the bag's contents for the source, which wasn't too hard to find. The fitted and top sheet both had a large amount of greenish vomit residue. Unfortunately, the experience induced a similar reaction in me, and I promptly puked all over the potential crime scene evidence. Not my finest hour. I shoved the now-tainted sheets back into the trash bag and lugged all three bags back to my apartment. If the murderer returned to the scene of the crime, I wanted them to know someone was onto them.

There was so much new information to process. I went to get my notebook from the bedroom, but it was nowhere to be found. And I had a feeling I knew just who had taken it.

My phone buzzed. It was a text from Detective Johannes:

AJ alive, but comatose. Kings Hospital, 5th floor

I would deal with the missing notebook later. I called a taxi and headed out to the hospital. Twenty minutes later, I arrived at Kings Hospital. There were two high-rise buildings connected by one of those sky walkways that looked like it was designed by a fan of the Jetsons.

I texted Detective Johannes:

which building?

Minutes passed, and he didn't respond. On a hunch, I went with the building on the left and optimistically took the large elevator up to the fifth floor.

I peered down the brightly lit hallway and spotted what looked like a Johannes-shaped man standing guard outside one of the hospital rooms. I waved and was relieved to see the Detective Johannes-shape wave back. He was further away than I thought, and the freshly waxed floors squeaked as I walked the long hallway. Quite an entrance I was making.

Detective Johannes greeted me with a handshake. "Luella. So soon."

He showed me into the hospital room. There were two single beds divided by a blue checkered curtain. An older man slept on the bed closest to the door. We tiptoed past so as not to wake him.

Johannes peeled back the blue curtain to reveal AJ lying in the hospital bed by the window. He had six different tubes going in and out of his tattooed arms. His complexion was gray. I could see ligature marks on his wrists from where the rope had been tied. His eyes were closed, but he was breathing. The heart monitor was beeping regularly. I let out a deep sigh of relief. I could see it with my own eyes: AJ was alive.

Johannes stood at the foot of the bed and spoke in an almost whisper.

"The doctors say he's stabilized, but nobody's tried talking to him. He hasn't woken up yet."

I nodded and took a seat on the vinyl chair next to the bed. Johannes tugged at his mustache.

"I'm gonna go make some calls. If you need me, I'll be just outside," he said and stepped out of the room.

I had a theory, but it felt far-fetched. I didn't want to ruin my credibility with Johannes, so I waited until I heard his shoes squeaking far down the hallway. Then I lifted AJ's hospital gown around his midsection and gasped. His navel was covered in a hospital bandage, just as I'd suspected. He'd been sliced, just like David G. The killer had something of a trademark.

AJ's eyes stayed closed and his breathing remained steady. I watched his chest move up and down, up and down, up and down. I sat there with AJ for close to an hour, texting Lauren periodically to let her know he was stable. I must have fallen asleep in the chair because I woke with a furious tailbone and a scalp on fire. I checked my phone — three texts and a missed call from Ethan.

Hey where are you?

Can we talk?

you ok?

I called him back, and he picked up before the first ring had ended.

"Hey, what's up?" I whispered.

"We gotta talk. Where are you?" he asked.

"Hospital, with AJ. What's up?"

"He's alive?" Ethan's voice hitched, and he cleared his throat. "Well, when can you be back?"

I looked at the time. It was 3 p.m. "By 6," I said. I needed to do a few things first.

"Okay meet at my place at 6. I'm in 8A," he said.

Hanging up, I wondered what in Ethan's world could be so urgent. I stood up to go, not realizing I'd sweat through my shirt. What was left of my burnt back skin had formed a bond with the vinyl of the hospital chair. The pain that ensued caused me to erupt in a series of expletives so loud, I accidentally woke the sleeping old man in the bed next to AJ's. As I shuffled out of the room, I found him sitting up in bed and giving me the finger.

"Sorry! Feel better!" I whispered.

Johannes was still sitting in the fifth floor waiting room when I walked out. He asked if I needed a ride back. I said, "Sure." He drove a policeman's standard issue Dodge Charger. Just as I got in the car, Johannes grabbed an old fast food bag that'd been sitting on the passenger seat and shoved it into the glove compartment. And they say chivalry is dead!

We both buckled up, and Johannes nodded over at me.

"You know, I got a guy who could fix that front tooth for you. I'll send you his info."

I told you, nobody ever misses a missing front tooth.

I brought up AJ's navel incision. He said he'd check his system for a matching *modus operandi*. I doubted he'd find one. Johannes did, too. "If I had to guess, I'd say we are dealing with a very inexperienced killer," he said. "That means he might slip up, but until we catch him, he'll be unpredictable."

"He?" I asked.

Johannes shrugged his shoulders. "Maybe."

I looked around the car's interior. I'd actually never been in the front of a police car before. "Know much about cars?"

"Sure. What do you need to know?" he asked.

I pulled out the car key I'd taken from Stephanie's bedside table.

"What's this for?"

Johannes took the key, turned it around, and examined it closely. The top of the key was black plastic, and I didn't notice until then that there was a small logo engraved at its center.

"If I'm not mistaken, that's a Dodge Ram. See? Dodge." He held up his own keys next to the one I'd given him — the engraved logos matched.

He continued, "But it must be an older model. It doesn't have the lock buttons like the newer ones do." He handed the key back to me.

"If I had to guess, you're looking for an older model Dodge, maybe from 2004-2006."

What was Stephanie doing with a key to a 2006 Dodge? Maybe it was sentimental — a first car or something? But who kept their car key in a bedside table? Perhaps someone who didn't use the car a lot, if at all. Maybe this key was for emergencies only. Or maybe she was keeping it for a friend. I wondered how long until she'd realize it was missing.

39

Detective Johannes dropped me at my apartment building at 4 p.m., so I had two hours before I was supposed to meet Ethan. That Dodge key was burning a hole in my pocket, and I wanted to find Stephanie's car. I had a feeling it'd be somewhere in the crew lot. I made my way over there, scanning the rows of trucks and vans for the Ram insignia.

As it turned out, many of the vans had the Ram insignia. In fact, every single van in the lot was a Dodge Ram. I did a preliminary count — I could see nineteen Dodge vans from where I was standing. I wished I could identify the vans specifically from 2004-2006, but they all looked the same to me. Like Transformer mice. Luckily, I had some time. I would check as many as I could. The key might fit into one of them, and who knew what was inside.

The first row I checked had four vans. None of them were a match. The second row had three vans. Again, no matches. It looked like I was alone out there, so I took the opportunity to scratch my itchy head for a glorious minute. In a state of near physical ecstasy, I walked to the third row, and that's when I saw David N on his hands and knees on the hot, black asphalt. I watched as he reached his whole arm underneath a parked van. He seemed to be searching for something.

"Hey!" I yelled to him. "What are you doing?"

MURDER ON SEX ISLAND

He startled and jumped to his feet.

"Luella! What are you doing here?" He brushed off his palms on his swim trunks.

"I asked first."

He stood there staring at me for almost a minute. I was about to ask if he was physically okay when he spoke again.

"I'm looking for my contact lens. Lenses. Both of them. Both of them fell out," he stuttered.

"On the ground?" I asked.

"Yeah, I need to find them... so I can put them back... into my eyes." David N crossed his arms and nodded, then decided to look directly into the sun.

"Uh-huh."

"What's up with your tooth?" he asked, pointing at my mouth.

"You're nearsighted?" I asked.

David N shrugged. "I guess. Hey, what's that?" he asked, pointing at the key in my hand. He operated like a toddler learning to speak.

"John lent me a van." Not my best lie, not my worst.

He stepped closer to me. I could smell his sweat.

"Which van?" he asked, holding out his hand for the key. I doubled down on my grip.

"Maybe this one?" I said, sticking the key into the van door he'd been looking below.

"I don't think so," he said. His voice cracked midway through his sentence.

The key fit. I turned it to the left and heard the lock click open. I glanced at David N as I held the door slightly ajar.

"Guess it was this one!" I said.

He furrowed his brow. "Where'd you say you got that key again?"

"John," I said.

He knew I was lying now, and his face turned ashen.

"I gotta go!" he shouted as he ran off in the direction of the apartment building. He moved so fast, he formed little clouds of sand in his wake.

Once David N was out of sight, I looked below the van for myself. There was nothing as far as I could see. What was he looking for, I wondered. I didn't know him to wear contacts, and if he did, one would think dropping them on the hot asphalt would be an endgame.

There was something about my entering this van, in particular, that set him off. I opened the driver's side door all the way, and climbed inside. It was exceedingly warm, so much so, the air inside the van had an almost wavy quality. There was a white leaf-shaped air freshener hanging from the rearview mirror. It made the van smell like coconut, in the worst way. The interior looked like all the other vans I'd been in during my time on *Sex Island*. Dark gray leather. Sandy car mats.

There was nothing in the glove compartment. A mostly empty plastic water bottle sat in the cup holder. I felt the bottle. The water inside was warm — it must've been sitting in there for a while. Underneath the water bottle, I found a wadded up napkin from Scoopy's and an old grocery store receipt for eggs, yogurt, frozen blueberries, and Gatorade.

I looked down at the passenger-side car mat and saw what looked like a sandy footprint, men's size 10 or 11. I crawled back through the van's three rows of hot leather seats. There was nothing remarkable back there. From what I could tell, this was just another production van. But why would Stephanie keep the key in her bedside table, and why was David N acting so oddly when I got in? The Scoopy's napkin was throwing me for a loop. Was John somehow involved in this, too?

Then I got to the trunk. There, resting on its side, was a mostly full gallon jug of Prestone Antifreeze. The same brand I'd seen in the trash bag on top of AJ's unconscious body. There was always the chance that it was here for car maintenance, but I didn't think so. I had a strong feeling the contents of that jug had taken the life of one man and might soon take another.

I scoured the van for any other corroborating evidence. Maybe a loose piece of John's hair, or a button from David G's shirt, David N's lost contact lenses. I found nothing else. I looked at the time and realized an hour had past. I was so thirsty, my mouth felt like tissue paper. For a second I considered drinking what was left of that warm plastic water bottle.

I finally pried my skin off the leather seat (they had become one), locked the van, and trudged the short walk back to the apartment building drenched in sweat. In the entryway, the air-conditioning hit me the moment I entered, and it was glorious. I couldn't wait to get something cool to drink. A lemonade! A Wild Cherry Pepsi! Maybe an Arnold Palmer! But of course, I was intercepted at the elevator bank.

Blair stood before me with her hands on her hips. She had her hair up in what I could only describe as "pineapple style." Her eyes narrowed.

"I heard you saw AJ. He's, like, *in* the hospital?"

I nodded slowly, not sure what her question meant. I couldn't stop picturing her naked on a horse. I shuddered.

She shook her head in disbelief. "Okay, so, like, spill! How is he?"

"He's stabilized."

"Ew!" she said, pointing at my mouth. "What's wrong with your tooth?"

"Someone pushed me," I said slowly. I searched her eyes for any sign of guilt. Nothing. "You were the last to see AJ," I said.

"I don't know what you're talking about. Anyway, you need to fix that tooth. It's making me feel sad." She moved aside to let me pass. I decided to switch my approach.

"I know what you did with him," I said. And with that, I walked past her to the elevator bank, pushed the up button, and the elevator doors opened right on cue. Hell yeah! I walked in and didn't look back. I knew she'd follow me into the elevator, completely flabbergasted. I pushed the button for two and looked straight ahead. Blair stood next to me with her mouth agape.

"Listen, we had sex, okay? Is that such a crime?!" Blair's voice was raised.

"Depends," I said flatly. "When?"

"I don't know! Sometime Wednesday. Maybe, like, 5:45 p.m.? I didn't look at a clock! But the sun was still out!"

"Can you prove it?" I asked.

She let out a loud exhale. "Ugh, you're so annoying! Nate will back me up!"

Earlier in the season, I remembered something went down between Nate and Blair and David G, something involving a rim job gone wrong, but the details were hazy at the moment. The elevator dinged. We'd arrived on two. Blair followed me as I headed for the pantry. I drank three bottles of water one right after the other. After the third bottle, I heard myself let out an audible "ahhh!" Blair looked at me like I was some kind of animal.

I wiped my mouth and burped loudly. Blair winced.

"So Nate, huh?" I asked.

"I tell him everything. That's our deal. Whenever I want someone else, I just tell him, and he's cool with it..." Toward the end of her sentence, she'd trailed off. Did she lack conviction? She looked from side to side, then in a hushed tone asked me, "Hey, can we go up to the roof real quick?"

The roof? Where the hell was the roof?! Okay, I knew on an academic level where the roof was, but why didn't anybody tell me this place had a roof?! We went back to the elevators and Blair pushed the RF button with a long, pointy, purple fingernail. I'd been living in that building for over a week and had never seen that button before. I realized that time I ran into George Striker on the elevator, it was very possible he was coming from the roof.

When the elevator doors opened next, it was directly onto a tropical paradise. It looked like heaven. Every surface was covered in lush vegetation. There were big, earthenware pots overflowing with flowers in bright reds and deep blues and loud purples. Up here, the air smelled green and salty. I realized I was breathing deeply for the first time in days. Blair led us through a windy path to a nearly hidden bench. She did another loop around to make sure nobody else was up there, then sat down next to me.

"Nate's a great guy, don't get me wrong," Blair whispered. "Sometimes he just loses his chill. Not often! But like, when I saw AJ, we immediately had this spiritual connection. Sorry if you liked him, but what we had was undeniable. It wasn't like show sex, it was like real sex. You know what I mean?"

My brain was working overtime to keep up.

She went on. "So that afternoon I told Nate that I was gonna have sex with AJ, and Nate seemed fine with it, but then an hour later he was completely unhinged. He kicked a hole in his wall. It was scary, for real. He was like, "Don't do it, I can't take it anymore!" Shit like that."

I blinked. "So, what'd you do?"

"I told him that I was gonna have sex with AJ, that he's a grown-up, and that he can deal with it."

"Why are you telling me this?" I asked.

"Because I think Nate is the reason AJ's in the hospital." I saw her lower lip quiver. "And I think whatever happened to David G, it's totally possible Nate did that, too."

40

I knew it was time to meet Ethan so I left Blair on the roof. Nate, Nate, Nate. Why hadn't I considered Nate? Why had he been hiding with Stephanie and David N in David N's trailer? I'd have to pay him a visit after this talk with Ethan. I took the elevator back down to eight and knocked twice on Ethan's door.

"It's open!" he yelled from inside.

I walked in to find Ethan sitting on his couch wearing only a trench coat. I must've looked confused.

"Come in, I'll explain," he said. "Shut the door."

I was surprised to find Ethan's place so tastefully designed. It was brighter than the other apartments I'd seen in the complex. I realized he'd taken off the standard issue blinds and replaced them with white linen curtains. He'd put down a large cream-colored fur rug that made the living room look both sleeker and more inviting. A white cotton throw was laid over the back of the couch. He seemed to know what he was doing, aesthetically-speaking. I stood in his living room taking it all in. So, this was the real Ethan.

"Stephanie told me I'm probably going to be eliminated on Monday," he said.

"I'm sorry."

"Yeah, it sucks. I don't have any immunities left, and none of the girls seem to want me anymore." He punched the couch three times. I tried not to flinch.

"It's not personal," I said.

"Of course, it's personal!" he said, louder than either of us expected. "It's the most personal thing!"

"I'm sorry," I repeated. I didn't know what else to say.

He took a deep breath. "Anyway, I've been thinking about what I could do after this, you know? What's my next step? Because I wanna make it big."

"Okay..."

"What the hell happened to your front tooth?"

"Don't worry about it," I said quickly.

He stood up and turned to face me. "Did you know I've always been somewhat of an amateur sleuth?"

My heart stopped, and I had to remind myself to keep breathing. I still hadn't sat down, and I was grateful for that. Easier to leave quickly.

He continued, "It comes naturally to me. For example, I found out who you were real quick. A random 30-year-old comes on the show as a wild card right after David G goes missing? It's pretty obvious what's going on. Your accent gives something away. And the wig — well, it's a bit much, don't you think? It's like you've got Staten Island stamped on your ass, which needs work, by the way."

This was not the same Ethan who held a cold washcloth to my forehead. He began to pace the room.

"The competition on this show is steep. You thought you could just... come here looking normal and old? That people would believe you're a regular contestant? Every female cast member has gotten at least $10,000 worth of work done, and they're all 20. You stick out like a sore thumb. Like — like a missing front tooth!" Ethan forced a laugh at his own joke.

"What's your point?" I asked.

"Well, I've been thinking about it. For my next thing, I want to do a reality show where I'm a hot private investigator, and every episode I solve a crime. I've already got a title: *Ethan P.I.* Do you like that idea, Luella? Sorry — Marie. That's your real name, right?"

I thought of the black envelopes, swallowed, and took a small step toward the door. He certainly had an agenda, but I still wasn't sure what it was.

"So, the trench coat...?"

"It's, like, my costume. What do you think? Striker's idea. He's developing the show with me." He picked a piece of lint off one of the sleeves.

"And the little black notes?" I asked.

"Oh, those were Striker's idea. Typical director, loves the *drama*."

"You and Striker wrote those?" I asked.

"Well, I wrote them, but just because I have better handwriting. It was his master plan."

"You and Striker are a duo?" I took another step to the door. At some point, I'd have to make a run for it.

"Striker's a sniveling nobody. I send him dick pics every once in a while, and that's enough to keep me in his good graces." Ethan moved closer to me. "I'm a lone wolf, and he's one step on my way to becoming rich and famous."

Just then I remembered the text exchange I'd seen between Stephanie and Striker, when she asked *Did you get her?*

"Did Stephanie know about this?"

"Stephanie practically begged Striker to do something. She thought you were messy and incompetent, that you were probably a super fan posing as a detective to get closer to the cast. She wanted you out. Actually a lot of people did," he said with a smirk. "By the way, did you know the ratings skyrocketed after David G's disappearance? Doesn't that seem like a weird coincidence to you?"

Looking around, I calculated how far I was from the door, the window, the kitchenette. The kitchenette was closest — it looked like twelve feet away. There had to be something in there I could use to protect myself. I made a mad dash, and that's when Ethan pushed me to the ground.

The wind was knocked out of me, and I lay there stunned. The left hand at my rib cage, the right at my shoulder blade. I recognized that push. I managed to get up to my hands and knees.

"In the flag challenge, someone pushed me," I said. I stood up, brushed off my palms and faced him.

"Yeah?" he responded, with a twinkle in his eye.

"It was you."

"Could be," he said, his mouth slowly forming an evil grin.

"You pushed me, then you pretended to save me. Why?"

"Someone needed to slow you down. Your little friend AJ wasn't dying fast enough."

This wasn't making sense. "*You* tried to kill AJ?" I asked.

"No!" Ethan let out a loud, hard laugh. "You want to know what your problem is, Marie?"

I wished he would stop calling me that.

"What's my problem?" I asked.

"You don't know what you're doing. You're a rookie! A clown! I read your little notebook. A list of *thirteen* suspects — wow, way to narrow it down! I've been here for over thirty weeks. I've seen every-thing, and you don't have a fucking clue!" He laughed again. "Are you gonna botch this like you did the Taylor Bell case?"

I slowly inched toward the kitchenette. "So, who did it?" I asked, my voice shakier than I would've liked.

"Tsk, tsk, tsk. Now, I can't just *tell* you that. Unless you were to... I don't know... meet me halfway? Make it worth my while, Marie," he said.

"You want me to pay you?"

"Half of what you're making. Then I'll help you nab her."

"Her?"

"It's obviously a woman. I mean, don't you agree? Poison isn't really a man's weapon. Don't they teach you that in social work school?"

I was speechless, and he continued. "Our *murdress* killed David G, then she tried to kill your little friend, AJ. I was doing her a favor by pushing you. You could say we rekindled our alliance. But now, I have to come clean. Guilty conscience and all."

"You're suggesting Tasha did it?" I asked. Something wasn't adding up.

"It's the truth. Give me half of what you're making and I'll hand over every piece of evidence against her. Then you can run home to your little kitty-cats," he said, getting closer to me. Only three feet between us. It felt like human chess. My move next.

I looked around the apartment. The area rug. The window treat-ments. Ethan had complained he wasn't earning enough on this show, and before that he worked at a gas station in Kansas. Where would he have gotten the money to redecorate a temporary apartment? Maybe I wasn't the only one he was trying to extort.

"How'd she get him in my bathtub if I was with her at a cafe?" I asked.

It was like I'd slapped him in the face.

"Just give up! Have the police arrest Tasha, and go home to Staten Island. The first *Ethan P.I.* episode done. Case closed. I'll give you a little shout-out in the credits: special thanks to the ultimate loser, Marie Jones!"

Ethan's eyes were bulging now, and I could see veins pulsing in his neck. He was breathing hard. Clearly, he was overcompensating for something.

Suddenly my phone buzzed in my pocket, and the room was so quiet, we both heard it.

"Who's texting you?" he asked.

I looked at my phone. The message was from an unknown number. All it said was:

Come to 2A now

2A was John's room. I made a run for the door. Ethan tried to block me so I kneed him in his allegedly ten-inch penis. He doubled over and let out an agonizing scream. I yanked open the door and ran into the hallway, nearly crashing into Isa. She was carrying a pile of clean bedding so high, she could barely see over it.

"Whoa! Watch it!" she called out.

My adrenaline was skyrocketing. "Sorry, Isa! What's all this?"

"Oh it's you. I'm sorry," she groaned. "One of the cast members needs new bedding, and it turns out, that's somehow my job."

"Who!" I demanded.

"Nate. Apparently he came all over his other set, and now he needs new ones. Kill me."

If Nate needed new sheets, I had a strong feeling the old ones had been thrown out with AJ in the trash room.

"Hey Isa, have you seen Max?"

"The sound guy? No. Why?"

"Tell him to meet me at Nate's apartment. And to bring his equipment!"

I ran down the stairs thinking about Ethan, Nate, Stephanie, and Striker. There was definitely a web, and I was close to finding out who was at the center of it.

I got to the second floor completely winded and hobbled down the hall to 2A with a cramp in my side. When I got to John's apartment, the door was ajar. In my experience, this was not a great sign.

I slowly entered John's apartment. All the lights were out. I heard someone softly groaning. Tentatively, I walked deeper into the dark room. A rustling noise made me turn around, but by then someone had grabbed me from behind, and I felt a serrated blade against my neck. After all this, death by bread knife. Wonderful.

I felt hot breath on my ear.

"You poisoned him!" a woman's voice screamed at me. Francis.

"Francis, let's talk," I tried to keep my neck stiff and steady.

"You want to kill John like you killed my brother! I took your little notebook as evidence! You kill these men and claim to solve their crimes. You must be stopped!"

"I did not kill your brother," I said as calmly as I could considering the circumstances.

"Look at what you've done to John!" she screamed.

She kept the knife on my neck as she walked me toward the bedroom where John lay curled on the bed. A bucket had been placed on the floor. As if on cue, he threw up as we entered the room. The bedside lamp was on but the room was dim. John looked more haggard than I'd ever seen him.

"Something was in the Jell-O," he managed to say before puking again.

The Jell-O. Phil.

I elbowed Francis in the stomach, and it surprised her so much, she lost her grip on the knife. She dropped to the ground, groping for it in the low light. I may or may not have kicked her in the head as I made a run for the door. I needed to find Phil.

Francis chased after me, but luckily I got to the door first, yanked it open, squeezed myself out, then slammed it shut on her hands. I felt the bones in her fingers crunch. She yelped, staggering backwards. Truly, I'm not one for violence, but desperate times calls for… you get it.

I ran down the hall to the stairwell, then climbed up the five flights to the seventh floor as fast as I could. I couldn't catch my breath and felt stitches in both sides. I desperately needed some water. I made it to Phil's door, and started knocking hard. No one was answering.

"Phil!" I yelled. "Phil, open this door! It's Luella!"

"Oh Marie?" I heard a man's voice say behind me. I turned around.

41

Ethan stood there holding a hog-tied Tasha over his shoulder like a sack of potatoes. He was still wearing that stupid trench coat. Tasha squirmed but her efforts had little effect. I noticed her mouth had been duct-taped shut and her wrists were tied in the same way AJ's had been.

"Come with me," he insisted in an overly saccharine tone.

Though every fiber of my being told me not to, I followed him and Tasha down the hall. I looked for any sign of Max, but no one was out there besides us. Nate's apartment was 7C. We stopped in front of 7A, David G's old apartment. Ethan swiped his key fob and opened the door.

"Ladies first," he said with a sinister smile.

I walked in to find David N and Nate sitting on the couch. I noticed *D2: The Mighty Ducks* was playing on mute. Clever, very clever. David N was slowly eating Cool Ranch Doritos. He looked up at me and winked. I felt sick.

Nate stood up, brushed his hands on his board shorts, and walked toward me. "So, what's this I hear about you doing some private investigating?"

David N stayed on the couch, licking his fingers. He had crumbs in his baby goatee.

"Yeah, Luella, we trusted you were one of us. But you lied. That's fucked up."

Ethan carefully set Tasha down on the floor in front of the TV as he spoke.

"I told you guys, her name isn't even Luella. It's Marie Jones. She's a social worker from Staten Island. And she's 29 years old."

Nate and David N erupted in a chorus of ew's and ugh's. I really hated these men. I looked at Tasha and tried to maintain eye contact, but her eyes rolled back in her head. Drugged, most likely.

"Have you seen Phil lately?" David N asked, jeering.

"Where is he?" I said with gritted teeth.

"Oh, he's in the bathroom," said Nate. "Maybe you should check on him." He and David N snickered like school boys.

I made my way to the bathroom, not sure what to prepare myself for. The last time I was in that apartment, when I saw the sweatshirt, the box of tea, the cereal, and the wet toothbrush, I foolishly assumed they were David G's. Now I realized they probably weren't. I remembered that the tea was PG Tips, which seemed overtly British at the time. Maybe Striker was involved, too? I tried to wrap my mind around what I was dealing with here. Three young men, presumably on steroids and Lord knew what else, had a woman tied up. And here I was, unarmed.

I passed through the bedroom, which was as I remembered it, for the most part. But there, on the nightstand, was a pad of yellow Post-it Notes. I hadn't seen those before. I thought of Stephanie's bedside table.

"Hurry up, bitch!" I heard one of them yell. It sounded like Nate.

I walked into the bathroom, bracing myself for something awful. Phil bloody on the floor. Phil dead on the toilet. But nothing seemed out of the ordinary. No one was in there. It was eerily still, until I pulled back the shower curtain.

There was Phil, lying in the tub with a big smile on his face. He was positioned just like David G had been, and because of that, his tank top had ridden up. I could see his navel, which was an outie. I realized in that second, I'd never seen Phil without his shirt on. Something clicked in my brain. The bellybutton incisions. Before I could register what was happening, he jumped up and grabbed me. I screamed.

"Baby, baby, baby! Shhh, it's okay!" He turned me around and rubbed my shoulders so hard I heard a pop. He held me close to him with his elbow hooked around my neck and dragged me back to the living room.

"Look who found me!" Phil squealed, using a sing-song voice I found unnerving.

"Good detective work, Marie Jones!" David N shouted.

Phil sat me down on the living room chair and held me there by my shoulders. My tailbone throbbed and I couldn't move much. He was stronger than I'd anticipated, and his grip was tightening. Nate and David N were sitting on the couch. I glanced at the muted TV still playing the *Mighty Ducks* sequel. Above a tied-up Tasha, Emilio Estevez was giving a heartfelt pep talk to the U.S. Junior Olympics hockey team. Ethan crossed to the center of the room and addressed the group.

"I got your culprit right here, Marie. Tasha's all tied up and ready to be turned in. Just keep in mind I don't work for free."

"He sure don't," David N said to Nate, barely above a whisper. Nate smirked.

Ethan shot an angry look in their direction. "What'd you say?"

"Nothing," David N said.

Phil addressed me. "C'mon, babe. Say thank you to Ethan." I felt his fingers tap against my trachea.

"She didn't do it," I said, holding very still.

"She *didn't* do it?" Phil said, pretending to be outraged. He really was a bad actor. "Then who did it, hon?"

In my time diligently watching *Sex Island*, I'd learned a few things about these reality TV stars. Mainly, if they were going to do something, they wanted credit for doing it.

"I believe it was a group effort, but…" I said.

"A group effort," Ethan mimicked me. "*But* what?"

"It was a group effort, *but* Nate was the brains," I said, maintaining eye contact with Ethan.

"Nate?!" Ethan cried, pointing to Nate. "That fucking idiot?"

"Hey now!" Nate said.

"Nate couldn't tie his shoes if they were velcro straps," Ethan shouted. "You spend practically two weeks here, and all you have to show for yourself is that *Nate did it*? You see? I told you guys she wouldn't figure it out! We could've just continued with the plan!"

"Hold on, I did a lot of it!" Nate insisted. "I dumped both bodies. One in her bathtub, one in the trash room. Remember, I almost got a hernia? Maybe I'm not the brains, but I'm definitely the muscle around here! You ask me to do something, I'm gonna do it right." He frowned and rubbed his bulging arm muscles. "And for what it's worth, I did much more than David N!"

"Seems like it," I said.

At first I wasn't sure why David G's body was put in my bathtub, but now I knew: the killer wanted me to see his work. They could've put him anywhere, but they chose the private investigator's bathtub. Maybe they thought it'd scare me off, but they didn't realize I've seen some shit. Like I said: Staten. Island. Divorce. Court.

"Hey, I did a lot of stuff, too," David N piped up. "I had to seduce Stephanie, who is *middle-aged*, just to get the car keys. I even wrote her love notes, and I hate writing! These guys wouldn't have all the antifreeze and shit if it weren't for me, driving all over the island paying cash at every auto supply shop! I did that for the brotherhood. I would do anything for you guys! Loyalty is king!"

"So, when you were looking under the van..." I said.

"Uhhh, I was looking for the key... to the van? To get more antifreeze? Um, you guys, I think this woman is actually pretty stupid. Should we just kill her now?"

Now I had the accomplices, but I wasn't done. I needed the mastermind's confession.

"So, who's the brains? Couldn't be Phil, could it?" I said as stupidly as possible. I even crinkled my forehead for effect.

Phil stared at me, a twinkle in those brown eyes.

"Ethan, I told you she'd figure it out."

Ethan sulked. Phil continued, "Believe it or not, I formed this brotherhood of gentlemen only halfway through the season. No offense to present company, but these guys didn't understand how to play the game. See, *Sex Island* is a game, and in order to win, you have to play strategically. I gave these guys a chance for a guaranteed win."

"I'm not in your stupid brotherhood," Ethan said.

"Fine. Ethan's technically our... what would you call yourself, Ethan?" Phil asked.

"Our cockroach!" Nate shouted before Ethan could answer.

"I'm a consultant," Ethan replied, glaring at Nate.

Phil nodded to David N, who took over holding me down by my neck. Phil moved to the center of the room. Ethan stepped aside.

"See, Ethan is somewhat of a hobby detective," Phil continued. "Once he found out what we were doing to David G, he wormed his way in through blackmail. We've been paying him for almost a month now, haven't we?"

"More or less," Ethan said.

Ah. So, *that's* who paid for those nice linen curtains.

"I don't understand," I said. If I learned anything from *Sex Island*, it was to always get multiple takes.

Phil groaned. "Babe, keep up. As the weeks went on, it became very clear to me that David G was set to win. So, I needed to take him out. Are you following?"

I nodded.

"But I couldn't do it by myself. It was too risky," Phil continued. "Then David G went and gave a rim job to Nate's girl, Blair. Bam! Suddenly Nate hated him, too. And David N... well, I'd also want to kill someone if he shared my name and was better than me in every measurable way. Ethan caught on to us, so I brought him on board. A quarter of the prize money in exchange for information and discretion. Better to have your enemies close, right?"

Ethan rolled his eyes.

"Plus the ratings went up a lot once David G went missing! All of us are already super famous!" Nate added.

"Right, well… Kill the star, and the show takes off. Not such a high price to pay. I hope you boys appreciate what I've done. Fame is not so easy to come by these days," Phil said.

"Yeah, yeah, yeah…" Nate muttered.

"You killed David G," I said.

"It was a group effort, but yes, you're looking at the idea guy. Do you know how easy it is to poison someone with antifreeze? If it's a low enough dose, nobody knows what's going on until it's too late. The symptoms could just as easily be from a hangover. With that woo-woo Sheila as our medic, it was a cakewalk." He winked at me.

"The thing about poison is, people always assume it's the wife or the girlfriend. Hence, our gal Tasha over here," Phil said, nudging her with his foot. Tasha was pretty much unconscious by now.

"So, you couldn't win just by being yourself, huh?" I interjected.

"You know, you're missing a tooth," Phil replied, condescendingly.

"You had to drag all these beta males into your plan…" I continued.

"Hey, I'm no beta!" Ethan yelled.

"We're not fucking beta males!" Nate and David N said almost in unison.

"Was it a confidence issue, Phil?" I asked. My social work degree was really paying off now.

Phil shook his head. "Listen, I know I'm fucking hot, but I can't compete with a male nurse, okay? Nobody can. Besides, I deserved to win after everything I'd been through."
"What have you been through?" I asked.

"What have I been through?" Phil screamed. "What *haven't* I been through? You saw my childhood photo that was going around the internet. I was hideous! My own mother called me ugly and disgusting!"

"The photo in your trailer... that's your mother?"

"How'd you see that?" he snapped.

I shrugged.

"Luella, do you know what happens when you win a show like *Sex Island*?" Phil paused to collect himself. "Everyone on earth thinks you're *somebody* for once in your fucking life!"

"Why'd you try to kill AJ?" I asked.

Phil sighed loudly. "Listen, what happened to AJ was unfortunate. A casualty of war, if you will. Once Ethan figured out who you were, I knew the producers would keep you on until you solved this thing, which meant, essentially, immunity for you and whoever you picked to be your lover."

So, he was wooing me for immunity. Hearing him say it out loud kinda stung, but I couldn't dwell on it. "How'd you actually do it?" I asked.

Phil smiled then. He looked oddly proud of himself.

"At the beginning, I made nice with David G. Same with AJ. Same with you, babe. It started off with a few Gatorades here and there..."

The Gatorade! Of course. It wasn't Striker's coconut milk punch that poisoned me, it was Phil's Gatorade.

Phil continued. "Then some mouthwash in the bathroom baskets, homemade smoothies, Jell-Os, the syrup on the protein waffles — anything really that would disguise the taste and color of the Prestone. With AJ, we had to give him more in less time. Things got a little messy, unfortunately. I don't know if you picked up on this, but it really threw a wrench in our plans that he lived."

"If I was giving you immunity, why try to poison me?" I asked.

"Honey, don't be so dramatic. I wasn't trying to kill you. Trust me, if I was trying to kill you, I'd kill you. I was just *trying* to get you a little weaker, slow you down a bit, make your work harder, that's all. It's reality TV. Everyone loves a messy bitch."

"The dude knew what he was doing! How do you think his mom got so sick?" David N chimed in.

"David N, why don't you shut the fuck up? Anymore out of you, and you'll be next." Phil looked back to me. "I don't know if you knew this, but I'd been testing in the top three for the last month or so. I just needed that extra nudge to guarantee the win. I couldn't let some Staten Island fuck-boy mess with my plan. In fact, you should feel somewhat responsible for what happened to AJ."

"And he slept with Blair!" Nate added.

"Right, and he slept with Blair. Which is not acceptable in the brotherhood."

Phil spoke with a level-headed intelligence that scared the crap out of me. He turned and stared out the window. The room was briefly silent.

"Show her your thingy, Phil," Nate said.

Phil turned to Nate and glared at him. "No."

"Just show her," Nate pleaded. "She knows everything else now."

Phil shook his head petulantly. David N muttered something to me, but I couldn't quite hear him.

"What'd you say?" I asked him.

"He's got an outie bellybutton," David N repeated. "Before he got cast on *Sex Island*, all these modeling agents told Phil they couldn't work with an outie. Dude worked so hard on his appearance, but you can't push an outie back in. That's just science. So, at this point, the only way he can become a real model is if he wins. That's when the brand sponsorships roll in, and the money makes itself."

If someone told me when I started this gig that a young man would be murdered all because some guy's complex about his outie bellybutton... I just... no. Turned out Phil was scarier than Taylor Bell by a mile.

"You wanna see my outie? Here! Here's my big outie! Everyone, take a good look!" Phil screamed, then lifted up his tank top. There it was, just like I'd seen in the bathtub. It was your basic outie, right below his abs, protruding out half an inch. I wondered, did the modeling world really drive him to do this, or had he always been this way?

"That's why you cut both men's navels. To mark them," I said, trying very hard to conceal my horror.

"Well, Luella, when you say it like that, you make me sound like some kind of psychopath. Both times, it was a very small incision. I like to think of it as my calling card. Nate thinks it's cool. Don't you, Nate?"

Nate shrugged. "Yeah, it's okay."

"Oh, shut the hell up! It's not just about my fucking outie!" Phil yelled. "It's about respect. It's about coming out of this with something to show for ourselves. The four of us made a pact. We would make the show huge, then we would make it to the finals. We just had to ensure the right people were eliminated. Then I would win, and afterwards, I'd split the $50K four ways and that would be that."

The Mighty Ducks sequel had ended, and the credits began to roll. Tasha must've regained consciousness because she let out a groan.

I was wondering what these guys had in store for Tasha, when my phone buzzed. Suddenly, I felt all four men's eyes on me. Everyone had heard my phone. I looked to Phil, who slowly shook his head. My phone kept buzzing and buzzing. Somebody was calling me. Somebody who was not in this room.

"Give that to me," Phil said, grabbing the phone from my pocket. He looked at the screen. "Why is Isa calling you?"

He sent the call to voicemail and threw the phone across the room. It landed on the ground with a cracking sound. I winced. Should've sprung for the AppleCare.

"What are you going to do to Tasha?" I asked.

"We figure good old Tasha will play ball. We'll rough her up a bit, then she'll know what she needs to do to win come Monday. Maybe she'll even throw us her half of the prize money," Phil kicked her in the stomach, and she moaned. He walked over to the kitchenette and opened the fridge, where there were three Gatorades chilling. He managed to grab all three with one of his hands.

"I like you, Luella, so how about we play a little game? Two of these bottles have a lethal amount of antifreeze in them, and one does not. Pick one of the poison ones, and you'll provide us with the weekend's entertainment, dying a slow and painful death. Pick the safe one, and consider yourself lucky. You can celebrate by getting the fuck out of here and never saying a word to anyone."

Nate laughed, clapping his hands together like a circus seal. "Dude, yes!"

Phil slammed the three bottles down on the coffee table in front of me with so much force, David N's bag of Doritos fell to the ground. The seal at the top of each bottle was broken, which meant any of them could've been tampered with. All the liquids looked to be the same color blue. I couldn't be sure, because the sun had begun to set, and the only other source of light was coming from the TV. It was now a landing screen suggesting we watch *Mystery, Alaska*.

I swear I'd gone into this with a plan, but something must've gone wrong. I'd gotten their confessions and at this point, I was supposed to have backup. But there was no backup, and now I was being served my choice of chilled poison. I'd have to stall for time or hope for a miracle. I knew reality TV stars loved talking about their own ambitions, and I figured that might buy me just enough time.

I picked up the first bottle, then looked at Nate. "If you get away with this, what will you do next?"

"Well, I'm probably gonna become an influencer with branded sponsorships. I really dig start-up culture. Also looking to do some crypto ads, but I don't want to be paid in crypto. Cash only," Nate said.

I slowly unscrewed the cap. "How about you, David N?"

"Uh, I was thinking about getting into acting. I'm aiming to do one of those zombie shows."

I sniffed the first bottle, and something seemed off. I put it down and reached for the middle one. "You want to be a human or a zombie?"

"Zombie, duh," David N said like I was the stupid one for asking.

"I know all about Ethan's detective show," I said, taking my time to uncap the middle bottle. "How about you, Phil?" I sniffed it. Something was off about this one, too.

Phil seethed. "Luella, pick a fucking bottle and drink it."

Welp, that bought me about a minute. I grabbed the third bottle, opened it, and took the tiniest sip. It tasted like normal Gatorade to me, but that didn't mean much. I felt weary and achy, but whether that was from my earlier injuries or a sign that the poison was already eating away at my organs, I couldn't tell. Nate and David N both looked scared. Ethan's face betrayed no emotion. Phil's eyes lit up and a half-smile formed on his lips. His dimple was out.

"Now finish it."

I motioned to take another sip, when suddenly, there was a knock at the door. We all looked up. From the other side of the door, a woman spoke.

"I heard yelling. Is somebody in there? Is everything okay?"

I knew that voice. Isa.

Phil put his finger to my mouth and shushed me. He nodded to David N who tightened his grip around my neck. I was finding it more and more difficult to breathe. David N was strong for being such a skinny piece of shit.

From a criminal's perspective, I could understand why Phil wanted me quiet. However, seeing as I was probably going to die soon — either from strangulation or the poison Gatorade — I threw caution to the motherfucking wind.

42

"We're in here!" I yelled as loudly as I could. I don't know how much I actually got out before David N tackled me to the ground. Soon after, Nate piled on like it was some kind of rugby match. Somehow in the chaos, I managed to pull out my Luella teeth and kind of "chomp" David N on the shoulder. I heard him scream and knew Dr. Frank would be proud.

Ultimately, the weight of those two completely ripped 20-something men was too much for my frame. My lungs felt like they might collapse. Something excruciatingly painful was happening in and around my rib cage.

That's when Max, the sound guy, made his presence known. Any true reality television fan knows the secret to a good show is to be constantly recording. The best moments always happen when people forget the cameras are rolling. It's the only way to guarantee someone shows their true, horrible colors. Thanks to some earlier coordinating with Isa, Max had secretly recorded the guys' confessions, and now he was using his boom mic as if it were some kind of giant sword, which, I assure you, was not part of the original plan. I saw him swipe Nate hard in the back of the neck.

What I've neglected to tell you is that a few days earlier, Isa and I devised a plan. I kept quiet about it, because part of me was afraid it wouldn't work out. If I didn't solve this case soon, I feared whoever killed David G and tried to kill AJ would kill me next. And if that happened, I didn't want them reading my notebook and going after Isa.

We made a plan that late Monday night/early Tuesday morning she let me stay on her couch. I ended up telling her I was a private investigator trying to find out who murdered David G. She told me she was an experienced MMA fighter, she actively distrusted most of the cast and crew, and she would be happy to help in any way she could.

The plan was this: if and when I got the murderer to confess, she would be there as the first line of self-defense, and she would bring someone from the camera or sound department to record whatever they said. When I asked her for Max's whereabouts in the hallway earlier, she understood it was go-time. But there was a hitch in our plan. We were in 7A, not 7C like I'd told her. I only hoped Max and Isa would figure it out from all the yelling.

Thankfully, they eventually figured it out. Stephanie heard the yelling, too, and had grabbed her underwear drawer knife (I guess *that's* what it was for). The three of them arrived at 7A at the same time. That's when Isa knocked and asked if everything was okay.

Max opened the door with his key fob to see Phil pouring Gatorades down the drain, Nate and David N dog-piling on top of me, and Ethan screaming that he was innocent.

Isa proceeded to beat the shit out of David N, while Stephanie stared on in horror. Phil made a run for it, and Ethan followed him out. Stephanie eventually pulled out her underwear drawer knife and stabbed Nate in the ass. At that point, I had unfortunately lost consciousness, because I would've really liked to have seen that.

As luck would have it, Blair and Sarah heard the commotion, too. They were heading our way with "weapons," when they intercepted

Ethan. Phil, being the slimeball that he was, somehow outran them. What happened to Ethan was the greatest thing I've ever heard, so I will include the actual transcript from the police report:

> JOHANNES: *Can you state for the record what you did to Ethan Robards?*
>
> BLAIR: *I tased him.*
>
> JOHANNES: *And how did Mr. Robards react?*
>
> BLAIR: *He screamed.*
>
> JOHANNES: *Then what happened?*
>
> BLAIR: *Well, then she stabbed him with a cactus.*
>
> SARAH: *Yeah, then I stabbed him with a cactus.*
>
> JOHANNES: *Can you describe this cactus?*
>
> SARAH: *Well, it looked like it was ten inches.*
>
> BLAIR: *But it was really more like eight and a half.*

The poetic justice was, as the young people say, "chef's kiss." Ethan, Nate, and David N were arrested, but Phil remained on the lam. Tasha and I were brought to Kings Hospital. On the bright side, it turned out I chose the right Gatorade bottle. Maybe deep down, Phil didn't want me to die. Okay, I know, I know, and I *am* getting over him! I understand it's bad and wrong to have feelings for a murderer. On an intellectual level, I'm totally with you.

You might be wondering how this case was actually solved.

Psychologically-speaking, I was looking for a murderer who sought acknowledgment, power, and admiration, which seemed to me like a cast member. When I first learned about the antifreeze, I thought the murderer might be a jilted ex-lover; that could mean Tasha, Sarah, or Blair. But the bellybutton incision was significant. If you're murderous and you're taking a knife to your ex-lover's dead body, I would assume you'd choose a more X-rated body part to mar.

Tasha was with me when David G's body would've been placed in my bathtub, so at least I could rule out that she did it alone. And the fact that the toilet seat was up led me to believe I was looking for someone who preferred to pee standing up. The morning after David G had been found, when we were told there'd be an orgy vigil, I noticed Sarah and Blair were acting differently than the men. The two women seemed genuinely upset, quite unlike David N, Phil, Ethan, and Nate. It was as if those guys had googled "stages of grief" and went to town. I couldn't put my finger on it at the time, but their reactions to this horrible news read as false. I wonder if these guys could've gotten away with it, if only they'd taken some damn acting classes.

That night Ethan saved me (and it turned out, also pushed me), I noticed something strange between him and Phil. I'll remind you, these people were very bad actors, and Ethan's reaction to Phil's arrival was so bizarre and hostile, it was almost like he was *acting* mad. But it wasn't just their poorly-performed animosity. Going in and out of consciousness, I knew I saw Ethan in my bedroom. It kept nagging at me, just why he'd been in there.

When I found the list of people's apartments inside my case notebook, I understood why. I knew I hadn't placed it there, and I realized whoever did had done it as a bookmark. Ethan knew Phil was coming later that night, so he marked the page with the suspect list for Phil to see my progress.

Later, as I pretended to sleep, I saw Phil pacing in and out of my bedroom, giving him the opportunity to see the page Ethan marked. I figured they were working together, but I didn't know the extent. When I saw Ethan and Nate in the parking lot arguing, I knew Nate was somehow tangled in this web, too. David N was such a natural follower, I assumed if the other three men were involved, David N would go along with whatever they said.

I knew these four guys were working in-tandem. But who was the leader, the mastermind behind it all? When I got the call from Ethan earlier that day, I learned that the mastermind, whoever it was, was getting anxious. Because someone had told them AJ wasn't dead. Luckily, they didn't know he was in a coma. Only Detective Johannes and I knew that.

All this time, I suspected Stephanie was the ringleader. Now I know she was used as a pawn, for information and protection, just like Striker was. I did completely underestimate Phil. Maybe it's because he wore $700 flip-flops, or because he called the Statue of Liberty a "killer statue." Or maybe because some sick part of me wanted to believe that a 21-year-old reality TV star was actually attracted to me. Welp, now *that's* embarrassing!

I do believe Phil was subconsciously trying to get caught. If all you want out of life is to be hot and famous, it's a whole lot of work to keep murdering people who stand in your way. Anyway, I'm thinking of getting new business cards that say *Luella van Horn: The crimes solve themselves.*

43

SATURDAY/SUNDAY

Saturday morning, Kings Hospital was the go-to spot for the cast and crew of *Sex Island*. They put me in a room with Tasha. She was in bad shape, with a broken leg and a sprained wrist. Because of the drugs, she didn't remember much from the night before, which might have been a blessing.

The doctors told me I had four broken ribs and a severely bruised tailbone, for which I would require the use of an inflatable seat donut for the next few months. A self-fulfilling prophecy if I ever heard one. On the plus side, Detective Johannes managed to get me a new set of beautiful, white Luella teeth, for which I was very grateful.

Down the hall, David N shared a room with Nate, where they were both handcuffed to their beds. David N had two black eyes and a broken tibia from his dealings with Isa, plus a bite mark on his shoulder from yours truly. The nurses didn't think it looked human, so they gave him a rabies shot. Won't be telling Dr. Frank about that. Nate had a broken collar bone from Max's boom mic and needed fifteen stitches in his right butt cheek. Not too shabby for a four-inch knife from Stephanie's underwear drawer. Ethan needed to have a bunch of minuscule cactus needles removed, but that was an outpatient procedure. Afterward he had to spend the night in the local jail.

John got a room to himself, the lucky bastard. Apparently that Jell-O Phil made for me had a higher concentration of Prestone, and John had eaten a large portion of the stuff. His liver was in bad shape but he was awake. Right after Francis attacked me, John had gotten violently ill, and she brought him to the hospital just in time.

On the fifth floor, AJ still lay in his coma. Detective Johannes told me he had one of his guys stationed there around the clock, just in case he woke up and wanted to talk, but so far he hadn't woken up. I didn't want to imagine what that stupid brotherhood did to him before they left him for dead in the trash room. It's a sick world we live in.

By Sunday morning, still no one had seen Phil. Isa took the lead on a manhunt, and eventually one of the wardrobe ladies found him trembling behind a rack of clothes. Wardrobe ladies, if you're reading this, for that I'll call us even.

Stephanie made a bunch of calls to the network to see if it was legal to air the guys' confessions as part of the final episode. The network agreed, under the condition that it play over B-roll footage of the four remaining women running in slow-motion. This fucking show.

As I lay in my hospital bed that weekend, I thought about what drove people to hurt each other. Surely, it wasn't just about a bellybutton being an innie or an outie. Life couldn't be so cheap. I thought about beautiful young people with their whole lives ahead of them. I thought back to when I was that age, how fragile I was, how uncertain, how I just wanted someone to tell me what to do. Maybe that was how those boys fell into Phil's trap.

Deep down, I'm sure David G was just as messy as everyone else, but from the outside, he seemed to know what he wanted. He had confidence and charisma. He had star power. Maybe that was enough to push a guy like Phil over the edge.

In a lot of ways, I related to Phil. I've been overlooked most of my life, too, and at one point I got so sick of it, I became a private detective in a blonde wig. Phil thought killing David G would be the solution to his problems, while I thought becoming Luella van Horn would be mine. We were both so afraid of being uncovered, he as flawed, me as Marie Jones.

But there is something freeing about being confronted with your deepest fears. Those little black envelopes were alarming, but my only option was to keep going. To solve the case as someone who was not strictly Luella van Horn or Marie Jones, but a person in between, a person capable of being both. I imagine the next case will feel different.

Phil was so afraid to be seen as ugly, and ultimately that's exactly what happened. I wondered if, like me, he felt some small sense of relief.

44

MONDAY

On Monday morning, Tasha and I were taken back to set. Neither of us looked quite TV-ready, but we were both relieved to have an excuse to leave the hospital. On our ride over, I asked Tasha if she had any idea what those guys had been up to.

"I wish I did," she said, letting out a long sigh. "I assumed that we were all friends, that we all thought it was just a stupid show." Tasha sniffled, dabbing at her eyes with the sides of thumbs. "Shit, now I'm ruining my mascara," she said, laughing at herself. Tasha reached out and gave my hand a squeeze. "Bitch, thank you. You saved my life."

I squeezed back. "You're welcome, bitch."

Our van pulled up to the beach, and Isa was there to greet us with her clipboard.

"Good morning! Welcome to the season finale of *Sex Island!*" Isa had large bruises up and down her arms, but she looked happier than I'd ever seen her.

Isa, Tasha, and I made for quite the ragtag crew. Tasha was on crutches but we managed to hobble down to set — the same one I'd seen my first day, complete with the Hibiscus Arch. Max, the sound guy, gave me a microphone on a lanyard.

"Dude! How kick-ass was Friday? I broke my boom mic in half over Nate's head!"

"Amazing," I said.

"Oh man, I tried finding your porn on Sunday, but nothing came up. You gotta send me the links, okay?"

"Will do," I said, saluting him. Isa had told this guy I was a private investigator, and still he thought I did porn, too. I mean, there are only so many hours in the day, man!

When Blair and Sarah saw us, they burst out of their trailers and came running down to the beach. They squeezed us so hard I think I may have broken a fifth rib.

"Guess what? I tased Ethan!" Blair squealed.

"And I cactused him," Sarah added.

There were a lot of high-pitched screaming noises that followed. It was good to see Tasha with a twinkle in her eye again. I saw one of the wardrobe ladies heading toward me with a see-thru robe on a hanger. I made direct eye contact, slowly shook my head, and this woman made the cleanest U-turn I've ever seen. I felt pretty good about that interaction.

When Stephanie Hillson and George Striker arrived on set, everyone quieted, awaiting instructions. What would a *Sex Island* episode be like without any heterosexual sex? Like a king without his crown! Like... like a skunk without its stink! Even now, months later, I'm tearing up at the mere thought! Where's the Kleenex?!

Stephanie spoke first. "Ladies. I want to say congratulations for making it this far. Due to extenuating circumstances, you will all be splitting the grand prize of $100,000 dollars. Well, not Luella, but Tasha, Blair, and Sarah."

Blair screamed and did a victory dance. Tasha gasped. Sarah started crying happy tears then looked quizzically at Stephanie.

"Why not Luella?" she asked.

I was about to speak up when Stephanie answered for me. "Because she's a 29-year-old private investigator who was here to solve David G's murder."

"Oh," Sarah said. I watched as she took in the information, then smiled at me. "Hey, good work!"

George Striker explained that the day's shoot would be pretty simple — everyone would do confessionals, then he'd get some slow-motion footage of the four of us running down the beach.

"But I'm on crutches," Tasha interjected.

"I'm sure you'll make it work," he responded.

His British accent sounded less robust than usual, and there were dark circles under his eyes. I almost felt bad for the guy. He left Isa to deal with the cameras and was heading back to video village when I yelled after him.

"George Striker!"

He turned around and looked at me, surprised. "What is it, Luella?"

"The envelopes. Why?"

"Right. Well, I'm sorry about that. Might've gotten a little carried away."

"You scared me," I said.

"I figured you could take it. I heard Staten Island makes them pretty tough."

"How'd you find out?"

"Oh, Ethan did the research." He sucked his teeth. "You know, I really thought I'd found my true creative match."

"Ethan's not your match," I said.

He winced at that, but sometimes people needed to hear the truth.

"Well, stay strong, Luella, I know you will. Pip, pip, cheerio!" George Striker saluted me and marched off toward video village. What a wanker.

I tried to take in the details of that last day, as it was safe to assume I would never experience anything like that again. Since Phil and the guys were now in Detective Johannes' domain, I felt a cloud lift. The sun was warm, the breeze light and fragrant. I took off my shoes and the sand felt warm on my bare feet. I looked at the ocean — it was still that cerulean, magic marker blue. This place was far too good for *Sex Island*.

Sometimes, when I find myself in disbelief that any of it actually happened, I'll watch that final episode. It's only about thirty minutes long, short when compared to the hour-long episodes *Sex Island* fans have come to expect. It still managed to get the highest ratings of a record-breaking season.

The episode ends with a shot of Tasha, Blair, Sarah, and me, just like George Striker said it would. In glorious slow-motion, Tasha is hobbling on crutches, Blair's breasts are bobbing up and down, Sarah is sneezing for the whole shot, and I look like I really have to go to the bathroom. The audio of the guys' confessions plays over the footage.

After that, an unseen narrator explains how the four male contestants are awaiting trial. Real cinematic stuff.

The confessionals that day turned out to be pretty epic, too. Allow me to recap the highlights:

Stephanie (off camera): What will you remember about Sex Island?

Tasha: The sex. (Long pause) And the island.

Stephanie (off camera): What will you do with the money?

Sarah: Probably buy a skirt, or maybe a couple skirts. Some pants. A jacket. Uhhh. Actually maybe a house!

Stephanie (off camera): Are you better at sex now than you were at the beginning of the season?

*Blair: I *bleep* so good, people get hurt. Always have, always will.*

Hell, even I made the cut.

Stephanie (off camera): Do you regret coming here?

Luella: Yes. But also no. But mostly yes.

Months later, I watch the episode as Marie. I sit on my couch, surrounded by my two cats named after my two favorite meat dishes. My hair is brown and frizzy. My front tooth is chipped. I'm 30 and divorced, with an ever-expanding flat ass. I watch Luella van Horn on *Sex Island* and I think, *who the hell is she?* You gotta love a wig.

EPILOGUE

I don't think it's right to tell this story without mentioning what happened to everyone afterward. Sure, solving a murder can be rewarding, but it's not like these people are all fixed just because they know who killed the person they loved or lived next-door to or worked with. Most of the time, things get worse. That's why I keep tabs on the people I meet working cases. Maybe it's the social worker in me, not that I can do much of anything about their problems. Sometimes the good people turn out okay, sometimes the bad people learn their lesson. It's rare, but it still gives me hope.

A murder plot coordinated by four reality TV stars isn't something that happens every day (thank God), so as you can imagine, the case got quite a lot of press. Phil got a good lawyer and was extradited back to Wisconsin to await trial. Eventually he was convicted of first-degree murder, and got sentenced to 35 years in a medium security prison somewhere in the middle of the state. Seemed light, but that's Hollywood, baby. Last I heard, he was making a lot of friends in prison. He was known to barter juicy *Sex Island* stories in exchange for beef jerky and hard-boiled eggs. He always loved his "protein fix."

My love, my light, my outie bellybutton killer. I thought a lot about Phil in the weeks and months after the case. Was it really vanity driving him to kill, or was it something more sinister? Did he like having three secret henchman? And most embarrassingly, I found myself asking, *did he even like me?* I tried to track down his mother at one point, but I found out she died when he was sixteen. I do wonder if he killed her, too.

Ethan's lawyer took a brainwashing angle, suggesting Phil was a sex cult leader and that Ethan was just a pawn in his game. Maybe the lawyer was right. During the final remarks she yelled, "Tell me! What did he do wrong?!" three times in a row. It became a meme people use when their dogs sneak food off the dinner table. The jury determined Ethan was guilty of second-degree murder and sentenced him to sixteen years in a Kansas prison. Most recently, he's been doing Cameos for $75 a pop. He told some news outlet he plans to do one of those "love after prison" reality shows the minute he gets out.

David N was sent to an inpatient residential rehabilitation center near Fresno, California. Apparently he came from money. I'm sure he'll run for governor one day, and probably win. I did hear he finally shaved the goatee, but apparently, he made it worse. Sources say he's been rocking a pencil mustache, or as I like to call it, the Devil's Dash.

Nate was sentenced to twenty years in a Colorado maximum security prison. He became born-again and an active participant in the prison's Christian scene. Recently, he's begun self-publishing self-help books. I read the most recent one, *You Suck, Now Pray!* And hey, it wasn't terrible. I do kinda suck. And now thanks to Nate, I pray.

AJ eventually came out of his coma after two and a half weeks. His motor skills still need work, but he's been going to physical therapy three times a week and getting better every month. After people found out what happened to him, he developed a pretty large online following. He does a lot of those videos where he'll be wearing one outfit, then he'll put his hand over the camera, and then he's wearing another outfit. People seem to like them. AJ and I still check in every once in a while. I talk more with his cousin, Lauren. I think we're on the path to one day becoming good friends again.

Justin, the guy who got voted off after one episode, turned out okay. He now has an OnlyFans where for $15 a month, you can watch him dance in a pair of crisp, white Hanes underwear. He is now officially a model/actor/model consultant/*dancer*. I'm a proud subscriber.

Blair gave up show business to live on a ranch in Texas with an oil baron she met on a cruise ship. She works with horses now. Don't worry, I'm keeping an eye on her.

Sarah and Tasha got a spin-off show called *Girls Island*. It's kind of like *Survivor* but it's just the two of them and neither one possesses any survival skills. Sometimes a single rotisserie chicken will arrive by raft, they'll fight over it until they're both exhausted, then sit and eat it quietly. They just wrapped their first season, and I heard they got picked up for a second one. I'm happy for them.

Stephanie Hillson still produces *Sex Island*. Somehow, the show keeps going. I don't watch it like I used to. Now that I know the inner workings, there's something so depraved about it all, and not in the fun way it used to be. But young, beautiful people keep signing up, and now more people are watching than ever before. This season, there's a "no murder" rule, and I heard they stopped that whole open-door apartment policy. Helpful. Smart.

Last I heard, Stephanie and her ex-husband were trying to make things work. She still emails me from time to time with long apologies, insisting she "trusts women now." I don't blame her — it's the world we grew up in — but I have yet to respond. Maybe one day I will.

John was in the hospital for three weeks, and Francis stayed with him that whole time. They ended up getting back together and rumor has it, now they're engaged. John quit *Sex Island* and moved to New York to work on a little show called *Dateline*, ever heard of it? He and I keep saying we should get coffee soon, but I doubt we ever will. Nothing personal, I just don't leave the house much. Plus, I'm still kind of afraid of Francis. John likes to remind me she didn't actually kill me with a bread knife, she only *tried* to. Regardless, I plan to keep my distance. She did eventually send back my case notebook. I almost wished she would've kept it. Reading it back makes me cringe a bit... at some points, boy was I far off.

George Striker ended up falling in a ditch. Listen, sometimes dreams do come true. I know it sounds like a joke, but he actually fell into a four-foot-deep ditch and broke both of his legs. Sometimes when I'm feeling bad, I'll think about how Striker actually fell in a ditch, and the world seems all right again. He quit the show after the David G season and moved back in with his mom in Bloomington, Indiana, which is where he's from. Turns out, not England. Last time I checked his website, he was working on a screenplay about an alcoholic genius who struggles with a sex addiction. I'm gonna guess the main character doesn't wear a whole lot of shirts.

As for the crew, Max still works as a sound engineer on the show. I haven't heard of any pink eye outbreaks, so maybe he's improved his hygiene. Sheila, the medic, is still there. She likes to send me long articles about the power of garlic that are most likely written by A.I. I remember one of them said, *Garlic is the power of cloves together. Release the deep scent.* I always respond with a thumbs up. Nothing more, nothing less. She seems to find this encouraging, always starting her next email with, *Since you liked that last one so much...*

The hair and makeup ladies, Carla and Hannah, are still there, too. They've proven to be my most reliable sources of show gossip, and in return, I send them Girl Scout Cookies from the States. I'd say it's a fair trade. That's how I learned Isa got a promotion. She's now a producer on *Sex Island*. Carla and Hannah think she's going to be an Executive Producer by next season. I'm really proud of her.

Isa keeps herself pretty busy at the show. I'm glad she's succeeding, but I hope one day she'll completely pivot and become a pro MMA fighter or something. The woman is *strong*. She mostly communicates by sending me links to self-defense videos with titles like *TAKE THE PREDATOR DOWN IN THREE EASY STEPS!!!!* For her birthday this year, I sent her a pretty sick clipboard. I think it was a hit.

Detective Johannes and I still talk. He keeps promising me he and his wife will come visit New York soon. And I keep promising I'll come back to the island. Maybe one of these days.

ACKNOWLEDGMENTS

I want to thank some friends whose support made writing a book feel doable: Maeve Higgins, Aparna Nancherla, Gabe Levinson, Marianne Ways, Maria Bamford, Sarika Talve-Goodman, Todd Clayton, Ziwe, Julie Miller, Chris Duffy, Clio Chang, Rubyn Wasserman, Alyson Levy, Greg Kozatek, and my parents, Marilyn and Fred Firestone.

A special thank you to early readers: Mike DiCenzo, Dylan Marron, Ashley Brooke Roberts, Bari Finkel, the Gotham Writers Workshop with Carole Buggé, and the Murder of Crows writers' group: Gina Hagler, Scott Brown, Ankita Saxena, Jill Rappo, Margaret Cooter, and Silvija Ozols. This book would have been so much worse without you! I appreciate your insight more than I can say.